CHOICES

by

Rose Fresquez

ISBN: 9798601010238

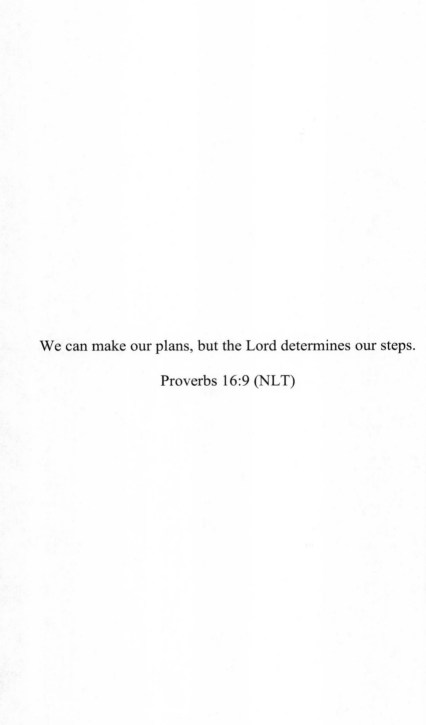

We can make our plans, but the Lord determines our steps.

Proverbs 16:9 (NLT)

ACKNOWLEDGEMENTS

I want to thank the Lord, my Savior. Without you, Father, there's no point in trying to do anything at all. It's my prayer that I can honor you with my words. I thank you for connecting me with an amazing group of people who helped support me in accomplishing this novel.

To my husband Joel, who works so hard to provide for our family, so that I can stay home and take care of the kids. I'm so blessed that we get to journey through life together.

To my children Isaiah, Caleb, Abigail and Micah, you fill my heart with joy. Thanks for the giggles, laughter and encouragement.

Unending thanks to my friend and editor, Elizabeth Proske. Your insights and wisdom have helped shape this story.

To Crystal Stewart, thanks for sharing your story of Tiger the cat, who was featured in one of the scenes in Choices.

To Lynn, Jess, Katherine, Amie, Donna, and Trudy, you ladies are so amazing for the time you invested to beta read and critique my manuscript. Thank you from the bottom of my heart.

CHAPTER 1

Zach Eron could probably wield a scalpel in his sleep. While a patient's survival was ultimately out of his hands, Zach often had to make quick, life-and-death decisions during surgery.

It was a relief to be presented with a choice far different from the critical decisions he faced daily. He already had a plan for the forty acres he'd inherited from his grandfather. That's why he'd taken a direct flight from the Philippines to Colorado Springs to finalize the paperwork.

As soon as he'd taken care of this business, he'd visit his family in San Francisco before taking off on his next adventure.

For now, he enjoyed the last spoonful of the best minestrone he'd ever tasted. After slurping the now lukewarm soup, Zach clanked the spoon into the empty bowl and shoved the dishes to the side.

His seat near the hostess station gave him a full view of the dim restaurant, and the steady blur of faces entering and leaving. He stifled a yawn and leaned back in the red vinyl booth, wishing he could just sign the documents and call it a night.

A sudden brightness nearly blinded him as the lights came up fully, illuminating a crowd of people nearly tripping over each other as they exited the restaurant.

Zach leaned toward his gray haired companion and raised his voice to be heard over the chatter. "What's up with the crowd? I thought in small towns, everything's quiet."

"Concert night at Ricci's," Wayne explained, his eyebrows pinched against the brightness as he dragged a piece of focaccia bread through the vinegar on the table. "The concert ended just before we arrived, and almost the entire town's here."

The entire town? An image of the gorgeous woman he'd seen at the same restaurant two months ago crossed his mind. Was she here, too, or had she left already?

A commotion near the door caught Zach's attention. Wayne's gaze followed Zach's, then he calmly reached for another chunk of bread from the cutting board. "Looks like Pete and Brent are at it again."

Zach watched in horror as a tall, barrel-chested man fiercely grabbed a lean, blond man by the shirt collar, and in one strong motion, shoved his face down on the counter. The blonde's face slammed against the wood and he slumped over the counter.

Several people gasped, one woman shrieked, and a man jumped up from his table, yelling, "Hey!"

Wayne shook his head. "Ouch. Poor Brent. He's no match for a big guy like Pete."

With blood trickling from his nose, the blond, Brent, swung a wobbly arm, but Pete grabbed the hand before the punch landed.

People clustered around the two men, focusing their cell phones and blocking Zach's view of the fight, but he could still hear them scuffling over the audience's excited murmuring.

Isn't anybody going to break this up? Zach squirmed in his seat.

"Stop it!" A feminine but commanding voice pierced the pandemonium. Instant silence followed, and every head turned toward the voice. The crowd parted like the Red Sea to allow the woman through.

Zach's jaw dropped when the woman appeared—the same woman he'd seen two months ago. Her smooth ebony skin contrasted sharply with Zach's fair skin. She strode with liquid grace and confidence in every step and gesture.

He was instantly reminded of a bedtime story his mom had made up when he was young, 'The Princess from Far Away.'

"Pete Haldem!" the woman called with authority, hands on her hips as she stared straight at the bigger, burly man.

Pete's fist froze in mid-air, but he didn't loosen his grip on Brent's wrist.

The woman folded her arms across her chest. "What will your mother think if you go back to jail?"

Silence.

The fury slowly drained from Pete's face and he lowered his fist, then released his grip on the blond man.

Brent jerked away and rubbed his jaw, then wiped blood from his nose.

"My nose better not be broken," he snarled, inching closer to his adversary. "Or you'll be in jail for good this time—where you belong."

"Go ahead and sue me," Pete sneered.

The princess hurtled forward. "Boys, stop!" She stepped between the two angry men.

Chest heaving, Pete took several steps backward and ran his fingers through his hair, his gaze still locked on Brent.

"Brent." The woman's pleading eyes turned to the blond man. "Please give him another chance. Don't sue him."

After one more glare at Pete, Brent adjusted the collar on his bloodied sports coat and merged with the dispersing crowd for a hasty exit.

With a relieved sigh, the woman dropped her hands to her sides. Zach couldn't help admiring the way the restaurant's subdued lighting illuminated her flawless face.

As if she sensed she was being watched, she spun her head over the sea of people and pinned her eyes on Zach. Unable to look away, he stared back. Their gazes held for a second or two, and his heart rate quickened.

The moment was interrupted when a man with a skin tone that matched hers approached her and said something before holding out his hand to her. A boyfriend, perhaps? She turned to the guy and accepted his hand.

As the man tightened his fingers around hers, the knots in Zach's stomach tightened as well. He could only hope the tense nerves had more to do with his exhaustion than with the scene before him.

Why was he bothered? He consoled himself that the man was probably her brother.

He had sat in this same restaurant two months ago, at Christmas time, on a silent, snowy night, when his eyes had collided with the same woman's. They'd shared an unspoken connection, which had brought images of her face to his mind from time to time while he was in the Philippines.

He'd chosen to meet Wayne at the same restaurant instead of the attorney's house because he'd hoped by some miracle she would be here when he showed up... and yes, indeed, she was here, if only...

"Hope those two don't kill each other someday." Wayne's mild observation jolted Zach from his thoughts.

He realized his mouth was still half open, and that he needed to respond. He wasn't interested in the guys, though. "Do you know that woman?" He pointed his chin toward the door she had just exited through.

The waiter refilled their drinks and cleared the dishes from the table before Wayne answered. Setting his water glass to the side, Wayne dropped his worn black briefcase onto the table.

"Chloe Love." He pulled out his glasses and slipped them onto his face. Unclamping the briefcase, Wayne sifted through several papers, finally pulled one out, and set it in front of Zach. "She's something else, ain't she?"

Suddenly not in a hurry to sign the papers, Zach shifted in his seat and settled back in the vinyl booth. As the chatter of voices faded, more questions about Chloe Love rose in his mind. He drew in a breath. "How well do you know her?"

Wayne adjusted his glasses and his warm eyes peered over them at Zach. "Most genuine girl in town. Almost everyone respects her because she takes care of all their parents in some category." He cleared his throat. "She's beautiful, too." His gray eyebrows fell back in place as he shifted his glasses.

"Yeah." Beautiful indeed. Zach nodded slowly, staring at the entrance, as if he half- expected Chloe to walk back through the door. "Who's that man with her?" He hadn't intended to ask that last question out loud, but it was too late to take it back. He stared at Wayne, waiting for a response.

"That's Noah. This would be their fourth date."

"Wha...wait!" Zach dropped his hands onto the table. "How do you know it's their fourth date?"

"My wife heard it from her hairdresser, who heard it from her client, who read it on Eron's Instagram page." Wayne pulled out a pen from his briefcase and set it on top of the papers.

Zach scratched his scrabbled jaw, which had almost sprouted a beard at this point, reminding him of the much-needed grooming after working around the clock with a flood of patients overseas.

Chloe was dating someone. His shoulders slumped, and he picked up the pen to sign the papers.

"Stick around and meet some folks," Wayne said as he accepted the signed papers. "Might get the chance to talk to a few people." He put his glasses back in the briefcase. "Don't sell your house just yet. You might like the town."

Zach doubted he would like anything about the town. Between gossip and restaurant fights? No thank you.

"My wife's a good cook. If you stay long enough, come join us for dinner." His genuine eyes held Zach's. "You've got my number."

"I gotta get to LA and visit my family as soon as I find a realtor."

Even as he said the words, deep down something told him he might take Wayne's advice to stick around. If not for any other reason than to get to know Chloe.

Chloe Love.

Just her name affected him.

Fourth date? Well, at least she wasn't married yet, and perhaps she was available to talk to him.

The phone rang, jolting Zach out of a sound sleep. He rolled over and pulled a pillow over his head to muffle the sound. After two more rings, the ringing stopped. *Thank goodness!* The caller must have given up.

Zach closed his eyes and tried to go back to his dream the phone's ringing had interrupted. Had he been in New zealand? What had Chloe been saying to him? His eyelids began feeling heavy.

The phone rang again, and Zach groaned in frustration. He fluttered his eyes open and looked around, confused by his location, then slowly his surroundings came into focus. Light streamed through floral curtains in the windows, a reminder that he was at his grandparents' house.

Right! My house now.

He reluctantly threw the covers to the side and crawled out of the warm sheets, swinging his legs over to step out of bed. He grimaced when his bare feet landed on the cold hardwood floor, and he tiptoed to the oak dresser across from the bed to grab his phone.

When he'd arrived last night, he'd been too exhausted to wander around the rest of the house. Once he'd turned on the heater, he had trekked upstairs and dropped straight into bed.

His sister's name appeared on the screen. He slid his index finger over it to answer.

"Addie!" He yawned.

"Where are you?"

Zach winced when his sister's loud voice pierced through the line, and he put the phone an inch further from his ear.

He raked his hand through his brown hair. He didn't need to look in the mirror to know it was a tousled mess. "Eron, like I told you and mom, would be my first stop when I returned."

His mom and sister had busy lives, but they still liked him to spend time with them at home whenever he was in the country.

"I know, but I thought you would start in LA before dealing with your house stuff," Addie said. "How was your trip, anyway?"

Feeling his feet go numb from the cold floor, Zach carefully sat on the edge of the bed. "It was good. I performed over 200 plastic surgeries on kids who were born with defects." The families of the children he operated on lived in poverty, so if he didn't treat them, the kids would live with deformities for the rest of their lives. "And, Addie, you should have seen the tumors on some of those poor people! There was this one guy…."

After sharing more stories of his medical escapades, he told her about the adventures he'd had traveling by boat from one island to another.

"That's amazing!" his sister said.

"Now tell me about you?" Zach invited, flopping onto his back on the bed.

Addie was excited that she'd been cast in a TV show, and was scheduled to do a photo shoot for a commercial for skin care products. Then she reminded Zach that their mom's birthday was coming up in a week.

"I doubt the house here will be ready in one week," Zach said. "But I'll go shopping for her gift."

Would this small town even have a shop that would have something to suit his mom's fashion tastes?

"See you in four weeks, then?"

He hoped it would be less than four weeks, but giving his family specific dates would mean pressure to get there at the designated time. "Yeah, see you."

He lingered on the small bed, debating whether to try going back to sleep or not.

He was up now, he might as well stay up. Tossing his phone onto the quilt, he crouched for his shoes. If he was staying for even a week, he needed to pick up a few items for himself while he shopped for his mom.

Rising from the bed, he grabbed his phone and plugged it into the charger he'd set on the dresser last night beside two scented candles. A fresh fragrance of cinnamon and pine emanated from them, filling the house.

He yawned, needing real coffee, something he'd missed while abroad. Since nobody had lived in this house for two years, he would have to buy coffee while he was out and about, maybe a coffee pot and a few groceries.

Instead of caffeine, Zach settled for a shower to wake him up. Stripping off his clothes, he noticed two towels hanging on the bar, tags still attached. Those hadn't been there the last time he'd come to see the house. He could only give credit to Leticia, his grandparents' neighbor.

When he'd stopped by the house two months ago, Leticia had offered to have the house cleaned by the time he returned.

"It will be clean so you can stay the night here instead of the hotel," she had said.

Zach had told her to write down the expenses of the house cleaning, promising to pay when he returned. He had also given her an estimated date of his return. No wonder he wasn't sneezing from dust like he had last time. He hadn't even spent the night then, but just the few minutes of the tour had sent him into a sneezing frenzy.

Stepping into the shower, he found a metal basket hung in the corner holding two bottles, a conditioning shampoo and bath soap. He gritted his teeth when he turned the knob and the shower sprayed cold water before warm water shot out.

Minutes later, he was throwing a navy blue t-shirt over his head. He ran a comb through his hair, avoiding a glimpse into the frosted mirror—no need to see his beard until he got a shaving kit so he could do some serious grooming.

The stairs creaked as he trekked down. A musty smell of old house and a clean scent of detergent and lemon filled his senses. A turquoise and brown rug covered most of the polished hardwood floor of the living room. To the left of the curved wooden staircase was the kitchen. The curtains had been replaced by blinds, not exactly the cleaning he'd expected, but that would give the house more appeal to sell.

Zach smiled when he saw a Keurig coffee pot on the kitchen counter. He sauntered toward it and admired the two baskets on the counter, overflowing with coffee pods, tea bags, hot chocolate and snacks of all sorts.

After setting a mug under the machine, Zach's stomach growled in anticipation at the scent of coffee. He ripped open a granola bar from the basket and strode to the window. Rolling down the blinds, he stared at the gently falling snow in the expansive meadow ahead. Even from here, he couldn't see the neighbor's house. He wasn't sure he liked this much solitude, unless he was at a retreat.

Despite the snow, he still intended to drive into town. His mom had warned him how tricky driving in snow could be. That's why he'd rented an all-wheel drive car.

Where to begin in town he had no idea, but staying in the quiet house all day was not an option. Perhaps he should stop by the neighbor's house first to thank her for having his house cleaned, and for the baskets of food she'd left him. Leticia could probably tell him where to shop.

He needed to meet people, like Wayne had suggested. Maybe he would stumble upon... *don't even go there.* He was only going into town to shop for his mom, himself and to find a realtor.

If Chloe just happened to cross paths with him today, it wouldn't hurt, either.

CHAPTER 2

With design ideas popping into her head all night, Chloe hadn't had much sleep. She'd wasted too much time last week competing against three other designers for a gig to make band costumes for a college in Boulder.

After learning that they had gone with a different designer, Chloe hadn't wasted any time rolling to Plan B–to raise money for Eron's senior assisted living facility by hosting a fashion show at the end of May, which was only four months away.

It was going to be a lot of work to pull off summer and fall fashions, but even more challenging to draw attention to the show from the right crowd.

First things first, she needed to get through today. On that note, she went out to start her Altima to warm up the engine, then headed back into the house. Her ankle-boots clicked on the linoleum floor as she stifled a yawn. Even a shower hadn't woken her up. An extra dose of caffeine was much needed today.

She followed the scent of coffee to the kitchen. With another yawn, she reached for her travel mug from the mahogany cabinets and grabbed the glass carafe, tilting the dark liquid into her mug.

Between her grandma's passion for cooking and her mom playing catch-up on parenting, Chloe did little cooking. Not that she couldn't cook, but the two ladies had made sure she was well fed ever since she'd permanently moved back home eight months ago.

A glance through the kitchen window revealed snow flurries gently hitting the ground. Two inches already! She could only hope her printed jumpsuit would keep her warm enough.

At least she didn't have any intention of leaving her boutique today. Snowy days in Eron meant slow leg traffic for businesses. Not that her boutique was busy, but on days like today, there were few customers.

For once, she was grateful for the slow pace, since it would give her the extra time to finish sketching her designs.

At the sound of a shovel scraping the driveway, Chloe didn't have to look through the window to know who was doing the manual work. She joined her mom in the living room.

Cynthia had squeezed herself into her wheelchair, a ball of yarn in her hands. Instead of knitting, though, her mahogany face, so much like Chloe's, stared fondly through the window, confirming Chloe's suspicions. *Noah.*

"Good morning, Mom." Chloe sank onto the recliner across from her.

Cynthia startled at Chloe's voice, but her smile brightened when she turned to see her daughter. "Mornin', sweetie." She gestured to the pastries on the coffee table. "Noah brought some breakfast."

Chloe reached for a flaky croissant and inhaled the scent of freshly baked bread. "He must have gotten up extra early to pick these up." The first bite melted in her mouth.

Cynthia's gaze was back to the window. "He's going to make such a great husband someday—or should I say, my future son-in-law?" She turned to meet Chloe's gaze, her smile hopeful. "Isn't he quite the gentleman?"

Chloe tilted the metallic mug to her lips and savored the warm liquid as she wondered how to respond to her mom. No doubt Noah was a gentleman, although Chloe felt like rolling her eyes. She knew where this conversation was headed, but her mom's face brightened with hope, so she held back.

"A great husband, yeah," Chloe whispered, and shoved the rest of the pastry into her mouth.

"I have no doubt he'll propose within the next two months," Cynthia continued.

Chloe choked on her coffee and stifled a cough. "Mama, I think you're getting way ahead of things here."

"Now that you've been on four dates already, something's about to happen. I can feel it."

Noah was a good man, and would make a great husband, but Chloe felt their relationship was still in the friend zone, too far from entertaining a marriage proposal.

"Good morning, Sunshine!" Her grandma walked into the living room, pulling Chloe from her thoughts. Her callused hands held a sewing kit.

"Morning, Grams." Chloe pulled up from her seat—this was a good time to get moving, now that Grandma was here to keep Cynthia company. "I've got to get to work." She bent and planted a kiss on Cynthia's cheek. "I left dad's medicine on the counter."

Chloe's step-dad had struggled with back pain for quite some time, and the pain had intensified in the last year, which had been a major factor in Chloe's return home, so she could help out around the house.

"Don't forget to take your vitamins, Grams." She gave her grandma a quick hug, then walked to the kitchen to refill her travel mug. She grabbed her coat from the rack on her way to the single car garage.

When Chloe backed out of the garage, Noah was scraping ice from her parents' Buick, which was parked to the side of the gravel driveway. Noah's knit hat and dark face were dusted with snow, his breath frosty in front of his face as his strong arms worked the scraper.

He smiled and stopped working when Chloe's Altima drew near. Cold air blasted her cheek when she rolled down the window and slowed to greet him.

Setting the scraper on the ground, Noah reached Chloe's car in three long strides, and his gloved fingers patted her car before he crouched at her window. Steam rose from his mouth when he spoke. "Are you ready to get those summer designs going today?"

She didn't have to tell him about the sleepless night and the designs she'd already sketched in the wee hours of the morning. She smiled instead. "Yes, I'm ready. That's why I'm so grateful for your help shoveling. I'm so…"

"We've already talked about you not thanking me for helping your family. I love doing that."

She still made sure to express her appreciation, which never felt like enough. She didn't have time to shovel this morning, but she'd not stressed about it since Noah had been shoveling lately whenever it snowed. "You're the best."

His brown eyes warmed under the white snow that coated his eyelids. Ignoring her compliment, he said, "I'm sorry you didn't get that job, but it's their loss." He spoke sincerely, the way he always did with her and everyone else. Noah had been confident that Chloe would get the gig, since he'd been asking daily.

"Thanks, Noah."

Acknowledging Noah's promise to stop by her workplace sometime during the day, Chloe waved at him and drove off.

She couldn't have kept up with mowing and shoveling the four acre lot on top of taking care of her disabled parents. With her mom in a wheelchair and her dad's intense back pain, Chloe had decided to open a boutique close by, using her savings from her previous job in Boston.

If she could only get a grip on her raging feelings, she might feel more at home. From time to time, Chloe wrestled with a mix of emotions—mostly about her relationship with Noah. After several months of him helping her family, and after weeks of his persistence, she'd relented to one date, then another, and now it had been four.

She figured twenty-eight wasn't a bad age to pursue a relationship, especially with Noah being one of the most eligible bachelors Eron had—handsome and hardworking. She liked him a lot, but was she in love with him? Even four dates with him hadn't given her a definite answer.

Maybe she was thinking too much. She set thoughts of Noah aside as she arrived on Main Street with its row of shops.

The early morning sky was dark gray, but all year long, garlands of Christmas lights lit up the street. Shops were still closed for business at this hour, and the town was quiet except for the occasional car, plus the sound of wind whooshing across the barren treetops. A drift of snow swirled in a glittering spiral, creating a perfect winter scene.

Chloe's shop was at the end of the street, a two story Victorian building she leased from her Japanese landlord. She savored the crisp smell of uncut fabric and new clothing as she settled in one of the two rooms she'd designated as her creative areas.

Hoping to be productive for the next two hours before her associate Jules showed up, she retrieved her sketchbook from her bag and resumed working on the designs where she'd left off at three am.

She worked all morning, sketching more designs by hand, drawing and adding color when an inspiration popped into her mind. She could do most of this on the computer, but she found it more relaxing to do it on paper.

When her associate, Jules, arrived two hours later, Chloe wasn't ready to interrupt the flow of creativity that poured from her fingers onto the page. She skipped their morning meeting and stayed in the workroom until their lunch showed up.

"I hate snow!" Jules groused when her boyfriend, Hank, hung his dripping coat on the rack.

"It looks like it's slowing down," Hank said, his dark wavy hair clinging to his forehead from the dampness. He unloaded several containers of food from the brown bag and set them on the table.

Chloe had set up sofas and a coffee table for customers to sit and browse through magazines as they waited, but she and her two friends used it more often when they shared lunch or relaxed to chat.

The aroma of garlic filled the room and Chloe took an appreciative breath.

"Hmm, thank you so much for bringing lunch, Hank," Chloe said.

"It's my pleasure." He handed Chloe a clear container with two slices of cheese-cake. "Thought you might want that, too. I stopped by the cake shop."

Chloe's lips curved into a smile. "I might skip lunch and start with dessert instead. Is that allowed?"

Hank shrugged. "Anything goes in this small town." Jules' boyfriend had moved to Eron four months ago, about the same time Jules did. He didn't seem bothered by Jules' mood swings.

"What did you get me?" Jules, the same age as Chloe, inched towards the table, her blue streaked blond ponytail swinging.

Hank moved to plant a quick kiss on her lips, but Jules turned. "Hey," she greeted indifferently.

"I got your favorite pizza," Hank told her. "Ricci's had the time for a custom order this time—white sauce, peppers, and basil, no meat, just the way you like it."

Jules sank onto the couch and reached for the pizza box. "Did you bring me the wrapper thingies?" She rummaged through the brown bag.

Her boyfriend apologized, "They were out, but I'll go back and pick those up for you before dinner."

"What about dessert?"

Hank stared at her apologetically. "I'm sorry, they were out of the chocolate cake, too."

She grumbled.

"Jules, it's okay if you skip dessert from time to time," Chloe said.

Jules rolled her eyes.

Hank chuckled. "That's why I love you." He sat next to Jules and slid a hand over her shoulder.

Jules pulled out a slice of pizza. "Shouldn't you be at work right now, anyway?"

"Yes, I'm on my lunch break. I wanted to see my girl."

"Whatever." Jules rolled her eyes again. No doubt she loved Hank, but it was hard for Jules to express her feelings to anybody.

"Hey," Sofia said, pushing back her long blonde hair as she joined them from her office upstairs. The slender realtor was Jules' cousin and Chloe's friend who'd moved back to Eron three months ago when she fell in love with the town's handsome detective. She now rented a room upstairs for her realty business. "Is that how we treat gentlemen who bring us lunch?" She lowered into a chair.

Chloe went to the other room to grab her wallet from her purse, then returned and offered Hank some cash. "Here's my share."

Hank objected, but Chloe shoved it in the pocket of his button-up shirt.

"I'll take the money off your hands if no one wants it," Jules said before chomping down on her pizza.

Sofia also handed him some cash, which he accepted without objection, probably to avoid having another woman shove money into his pockets.

Once Hank left, the girls prayed over their meal, even though Jules was halfway done with her pizza. As they ate their lunch, Chloe talked about her pressing needs for the fashion show. "I'm going to need several volunteer models."

"I could ask Brent to be one of your male models," Sofia suggested her big brother. "I'll ask him when the bruises he got last night fade. By then he'll get over being mad at you for interfering with the fight—he said you embarrassed him."

Chloe didn't regret breaking up the fight. Although Pete was short-tempered, Chloe always seemed to get through to him when most people in town couldn't. "He should be grateful for not having a broken nose. Your fiancé took the hit for him last time, but he wasn't there to save him this time."

"That's what I told Brent, too."

"I love my cousin," Jules was back to business, speaking with a mouth full of food. "but he's too stuffy. He needs to loosen up if he's going to model your designs."

Sofia and Chloe stared at Jules, who was no different from Brent when it came to being uptight. Jules pointed her finger to Chloe, "Hank is your man, though."

Chloe pictured Jules' boyfriend in one of her suits and nodded. Although Hank's height was just average, he was good looking, and would fill out the suit nicely.

"Brent's five feet, eleven inches, and those well-toned muscles qualify him for the role." Chloe stabbed a fork into her linguine. "If he models one of the suits, he will be in his element, since he wears them all the time."

"I'm not a fashion expert, but I'm pretty sure we'll need to book a photographer." Jules reminded.

Chloe nodded slowly. "And a pro bono website designer." They brainstormed about the list of eight more things that needed to be accomplished by mid-May, until Chloe's brain was spinning so fast she felt the need to change the subject.

"That was so sweet of Hank to bring us lunch in such cold weather," she said, and took another bite.

"I think we all have great guys," Sofia added, brushing a loose strand of blonde hair from her forehead. "Trevor would do the same if he were in town. I know that Noah would, too."

"We all think that Hank is a great guy except for your fiancé," Jules said.

Sofia shrugged. "Don't take it personally. Being a detective, Trevor always goes by his instincts, but I'm sure he's been wrong a few times."

"Whatever!" Jules shoved the last piece of pizza in her mouth and chewed before she spoke again. "Speaking of boyfriends, has Noah figured out that you're just going out with him out of guilt?"

Chloe's jaw dropped open.

Sofia forked her pasta and put it in her mouth, her eyes glued to her cousin.

"What?" Jules flung up her hands in question. "Don't stare at me like I just said something outrageous."

"Of course I like him...and not out of guilt." The last word came out weak. Did she go out with him out of guilt? Fear to let him down for all the work he did for her family? She stabbed at her pasta.

"Poor Noah." Jules' ponytail swung as she slowly shook her head.

"Why do you call him poor?" Sofia asked. "Noah is the most successful contractor in town, handsome and now going out with Eron's golden girl, as Instagram calls her."

"We all know that Eron has nothing to talk about," Chloe said. "Not that long ago, you and Trevor were the power couple, still are until you get married, of course."

Jules rolled her eyes and crossed one leg over the other. "I still think you should tell Noah that things will not work out. Whatever you two have going on is temporary. Tell him before you waste each other's time."

The food suddenly lost its flavor. Chloe reached for her cheesecake container and popped it open. "You don't know what you're talking about." Or did she?

Jules arched her neatly trimmed brows. "Really? You've gone out four times and you haven't shared even a peck, seriously?…"

"Jules, will you just drop it!" Sofia said. "Not everybody kisses a guy after four dates. I was an exception, since I kissed Trevor on our first date, but I initiated the kiss."

"Look at us, gossiping like teenagers." Chloe spoke between bites of her cheesecake. "It's no wonder we're all still living with our parents."

"I'm getting married in three months, I got a good reason." Sofia pushed a fork into her pasta and stared at Jules.

"Hey, I just moved back in town," Jules said, arching her brows pointedly at Chloe.

"Don't look at me." Chloe pointed her fork at Jules. "I'm moving out in three weeks."

She polished off one piece of the cheesecake. She was stuffed and contemplated polishing off the last piece, but it was probably not a good idea. She covered it up for later instead.

Jules pulled it in front of her. "I'll take it and I can get you another piece tomorrow."

Chloe pulled it back to herself. The last time Jules ate cheesecake, she'd only taken one bite and dumped the rest in the trash can. "You don't even like cheesecake."

"I need something sweet."

"I'll give you a piece of gum instead. Otherwise, check with me in two hours. If I haven't eaten it by then, it's all yours."

"You with your cheesecake," Jules whined.

"You could just drive to the cake shop," Sofia suggested. "Or to the country store for a candy bar."

Jules muttered something under her breath.

Chloe smiled. "We better get back to work."

Sofia stared at her phone. "Oh boy, it's already one-thirty."

They rose to clear the table and threw the disposable containers in the trash. Chloe carried her cheesecake to the glass jewelry counter, hoping to store it in the refrigerator for an afternoon snack.

The bell jingled in the front of the shop and a wave of cool air followed. The three of them spun their heads instantly to the customer, who was rubbing his hands together to warm them up.

Sofia turned to Chloe and whispered. "That's your handsome guy from a couple of months ago." She waved at Chloe and turned. "I gotta get back to work."

"You don't have any work," Jules said. "Real estate is slow right now."

"I'm helping Brent sort through some of his business paperwork." Sofia trotted toward the stairs.

Chloe's gaze shifted to the stubbornly square jaw of the familiar man. Speaking of models, he was the perfect runway model, with just the right height—she guessed him to be about six feet, two inches. The dark, long-sleeved T-shirt accentuated his lean and well-toned muscles as he approached with an easy, confident stride.

In that instant, an idea formed in Chloe's mind–a suit, although the unkempt hair would need some attention for him to wear it.

She'd seen him two months ago, and last night at the same restaurant, she'd sensed someone was watching her, and when she'd turned, she'd met his gaze amongst the sea of faces.

"Hello." The deep voice drew her from her thoughts.

Her lips parted to respond but her mind went blank.

She assumed it had everything to do with the sudden euphoric sense of warmth and anticipation. The same reaction she'd felt two months ago, and again last night when they'd exchanged a brief gaze. She felt like sparks were traveling from his body to hers, and somehow her intuition whispered to her, that he felt the same way.

CHAPTER 3

"**H**i." Chloe finally managed to respond when the man's strong arms rested on the glass counter in front of her. She lifted her head and met his steady gaze, and eyes as green as the meadows Chloe had played in as a child bore into hers. The intensity in his look made her feel as if he could read her heart.

Chloe glanced away from the strong jaw covered in several days worth of stubble and stepped back. "Let me know if I can be of any help."

What was wrong with her voice anyway? Where in the world was Jules? Chloe spun in search of her friend, but Jules was already at the corner desk, seated on a chair, eyes on the laptop computer. Jules wasn't fond of interacting with people, which is why she'd claimed the responsibilities of keeping the company Facebook page updated and handling the finances.

The man turned his head to scan the spacious store stocked mostly with ladies' clothing designed by Chloe.

"Actually, I think I will need your help," he said when he turned back and offered his hand. "I don't believe we've officially met. I'm Zach…Zach Eron."

His warm hand was firm in hers. A brief handshake, but it was enough to ignite a spark. She sucked in a breath as his last name triggered a dawning recognition.

"Derek and Lydia's grandson is coming to town. It would be wonderful if he stayed in his grandparents house instead of the hotel," Leticia, one of Chloe's senior friends had said when she'd asked Chloe to find a house cleaner.

"As in, a descendant of Derek Eron, in the lineage of William Eron the town's founder?"

His lips curved into a smile. "That's what I've been told."

"I'm…"

"Chloe Love?" he tightened his grip before pulling his hand back.

She stared at him suspiciously, wondering how he knew her name.

His eyes deep green eyes warmed to a simmer. They were filled with mischief and adventure. He lifted a shoulder, not breaking eye contact. "Small town, right?"

This guy couldn't have been around that long. Otherwise, Chloe would've known, since word spread fast in Eron. She'd seen his picture on Instagram in December when they'd posted the name of the inn he'd stayed at.

It was a surprise they hadn't known that he was related to the town's founder—otherwise, that would have been mentioned on social media too. "Yeah, everybody knows what's going on in everyone's life."

He let out a low laugh that released butterflies in her belly. "That's what I've heard. So it's true?"

Where was the fan when she needed it? Except she didn't own a fan because she had air-conditioning–but wait, it was winter and the furnace was running. She wanted to fan herself with her hand, but had no idea how to do it without acting awkward.

Whew, any more of this sweating and she was going to need another shower before the day was over.

Where were we? Oh, yes!

"I have the guy section in the corner over there." She pointed to the area with men's clothing featuring a few suits she'd designed. "I also have some casuals downstairs."

He smiled. "I will need some items, but first I need your help in finding something for a special woman."

Of course he had a girlfriend he was shopping for. Hiding her disappointment, Chloe asked, "What is your girlfriend's style?"

He narrowed his gaze and leaned forward. "I don't have a girlfriend."

Embarrassed, Chloe's hand flew to her chest. "I... sorry, I just assumed…" *...a handsome man like you had one.* "I mean..."

"It's for my mom." He stared through the glass counter that held the high-end jewelry. "Her birthday is next week. Do you think I can ship something to LA and have it there by Wednesday?"

He shopped for his mom? "Let's see...it's Friday. If you use express shipping, it should be there by Monday."

His eyes suddenly landed on the plastic container on the counter and he stared at the contents hungrily. "Cheese cake? It's my favorite."

Without thinking twice, Chloe shoved the container towards him. "You can have it if you want. There are disposable forks and spoons over by the coffee table." She turned to point him to the forks by the coffee pot and met Jules' stare.

Jules rolled her eyes so hard Chloe thought they might fall out.

"Thank you!" Zach took the cake and moved to the corner to grab a fork. "If you don't mind, I'll walk around the shop while I enjoy this."

He spooned a bite into his mouth and his footsteps echoed as he trekked down the wooden stairs.

Jules was instantly at her side. Her button down silk top hung loosely on her lean frame.

"What in the world?" She slammed her hand on the glass counter. "You never share your cheesecake. I even offered to pay you back tomorrow, and you refused to let me eat it."

She looked around to see if Zach was coming back, then pointed a finger at Chloe. "A stranger barks cheesecake, and you cave in like a…a…un-believable." She shook her head. "Just unbelievable."

Chloe chuckled at Jules' seriousness.

Several minutes later, Zach returned and threw the empty container into the trash can. His other hand clutched a bundle of clothes that he dropped at the register next to the jewelry counter.

"How about you help me choose three of these necklaces?" He pointed at the jewelry through the glass.

Chloe pulled out four of her favorite necklaces and spread them on the counter—a sterling silver lariat necklace with emeralds, a white gold choker with a sapphire, a plain linked sterling silver chain with an amethyst, and an emerald stone on a gold chain.

Zach inched closer and narrowed his gaze as he studied the pieces. He tapped on the counter before carefully pulling two necklaces to the side—the emerald lariat and the sapphire choker. "These two," he said. "Can you try them on for me, please?"

She hesitated. "I've…"

"It would give me an idea of how they would look on my mom. Her neck is about your size."

She'd done this for clients before, she told herself as she fiddled with the clasp. To hide her nervousness, she asked, "So how long have you been in town?"

"Long enough for this to be our third meeting."

She couldn't pretend she'd never met him before, and his steady gaze dared her to pretend otherwise. The clasp refused to cooperate, since her hand was suddenly moist.

"Let me help." Giving her no time to respond, Zach reached behind her and his hands brushed her neck as he tightened the tiny clasp. She felt an instant breakout of goosebumps. Thankfully her arms were hidden underneath the long sleeved jumpsuit.

I'm going out with Noah, she reminded herself. Noah was a nice man, even though he didn't ignite sparks or leave traces of goosebumps, like this newcomer was doing without so much as trying.

"I assume you're a native of Eron?" He stepped back and pinned his gaze to the lariat necklace nestled against her throat.

"Yep. Born and raised." She wiped her hands on the sides of her jumpsuit before unclasping the necklace. She turned to call Jules to help her with the next necklace to avoid having Zach's hands brush her neck again.

"I'm busy. I think the customer is very capable of doing that," Jules said, her eyes never wavering from the computer screen. Probably updating the Facebook page, or maybe checking her emails.

Zach grinned at Jules, who wasn't paying attention. "She's right." When his smile fell on Chloe, it softened. "I'm more than capable of helping."

Of course his steady hands were more than capable, since the necklace was already sliding over her head. Chloe's heart thundered and she kept her eyes on the hardwood floor as she inhaled the musky scent of shampoo that lingered on Zach's skin.

When she was done trying on the necklaces, Zach requested the amethyst necklace, which was hand made by one of the local artists. Their hands brushed when she handed it to him.

He added the amethyst to the emerald and sapphire necklaces he'd already chosen, along with his selection of clothing.

After accepting his payment, Chloe wrapped the jewelry in individual boxes. "You can get a shipping box at the post office," she suggested. "Also, if you stop at the country store on your way to the post office, it has some neat gifts to add to your mom's package. She might enjoy some random treats, and it will add a personal touch."

He arched a brow. "If I'm going to any country store, I will definitely need a guide."

Chloe folded his jeans, t-shirts and flannel shirts and put them into the brown tote bag printed with the company logo. "It's a small town. Just stay on Main Street and you won't miss the shop." She handed him the bag, keeping her eyes averted, lest he read more of her feelings. "Two blocks from the country store will be the town hall, where you will find the post office."

"I'm still a newcomer, as you noticed. I could really use a native to prove me wrong about this town being as boring as I've seen so far."

It was a small town, and might seem boring to a city person, but not to the residents once they'd gotten rooted. "I could have my friend over there take you." She pointed her chin to Jules.

Zach stared at Jules briefly, whose focus was still on the keyboard. "I don't know," he whispered, his words for Chloe's ears alone. "Your friend looks like she would rather be left alone." Then he spoke in his normal voice. "Tell me there's no creepy lore I should know about."

She found it hard to hold back a laugh. Zach laughed, too. She could use a break after being stuck in the shop all morning. "Hey, Jules," she called over her shoulder to her associate, who refused to look her way. "I'll be back shortly."

Chloe reached for her coat and stared at Zach who only had a t-shirt with no extra layers. Did he even have gloves? She had to ask.

"I don't have any gloves, but I left my sweater in the car," he told her.

Chloe pulled a pair of black gloves and earmuffs off the shelf and handed them to Zach. "You're going to need these. Try the gloves on first to see if they fit."

He shoved his long fingers into the gloves. "Is this how you convince customers to buy your products?" His face held a teasing smile.

Chloe shook her head. "Only those who are underdressed for the weather." She zipped up her coat and wrapped a scarf around her neck, then slipped her fingers into her own gloves.

When they stepped out onto the chilly street, Chloe had no doubt that the town would have something exciting to talk about once they saw her strolling down Main Street with the newcomer.

Chloe carried the bag with gifts for Zach's mom while Zach carried the bag with toiletries he'd bought from the country store. He had bought caramelized nuts and two scented candles, which were Chloe's idea, to add to the birthday gifts.

They walked along the line of shops on Main Street, stopping to greet people from time to time.

"You seem to know the entire town," Zach observed.

"It's a small town." Of course, that was just one of the reasons she knew so many people. "Plus hanging out with seniors and being raised by one of them, you get to know a lot of people."

"I take it you were raised by your grandparents, then?"

"Just my grandma. It's a long story for another day."

He gave her a curious look, then opened his mouth as if about to ask her something. Thankfully, they were interrupted by another man who stopped to greet Chloe, and Zach crouched to pet the man's Saint Bernard.

Most of the buildings lining the street were Victorian, with new paint, while others still had chipped paint. Zach pointed to one of the historical buildings, his eyebrows raised in question, and Chloe explained, "That used to be the town's courthouse, but now it's the community center.

Zach nodded, then asked, "Does your shop keep busy in the winter?"

"Not really. This is my first winter with the boutique. Last summer seemed busy, but I was just starting the business and I had less inventory."

"What did you do before you opened a boutique?"

"I stayed in Boston after fashion school." Chloe told Zach about the job she'd gotten at a Boston fashion house before she'd moved back home. "It was nice for me to get away for a little bit, and see what it was like out there, but I couldn't stay away when my dad was in a lot of pain."

Zach seemed genuinely interested, asking more questions about her shop.

After answering his questions, she told him, "I'm hosting a fashion show to raise money for Eron's senior facility." Remembering all that needed to be done for the show, she glanced at her watch. "All the more reason for me to be making phone calls for volunteers instead of being out on a stroll."

"Consider me your first volunteer," he said. "When is the show?"

With his good looks and attractive build, she'd already enrolled him without him knowing, but she didn't want to put him on the spot yet, so she just said, "It's the week before Memorial Day weekend."

"I'll be gone by then, but I could come back for your event. What can I do to help within the next two weeks?"

"You're just here for two weeks?" She hoped her disappointment didn't show.

"I saved the realtor's number that I saw on the sign outside your shop," he replied. "Once I make the call and get the house listed, I can leave. It will be a bonus if I can get it sold right away, so I don't have to come back for more paperwork. I need to visit my family in LA before my next adventure."

Realtor? House? Family? Chloe's mouth fell open as the words registered. She came to a sudden halt. "You're selling your grandparents' house?" Her tone came out more shocked than intended. It was his house, and he could do whatever he wanted with it, but that didn't stop the ache in Chloe's chest. The house and property held several childhood memories for her. It would most certainly be sold to a developer, since no one in town could possibly afford the property.

She suddenly didn't feel like talking about the property, but she had to know where he'd been, and why he'd never taken the initiative to find his grandparents.

"What brings you here all of a sudden?" She resumed walking and Zach kept pace beside her.

His eyes fixated on the flurries ahead as he told her how he'd been surprised by the inheritance. "I did't even know that I had any grandparents on my dad's side still living."

"Didn't your mom ever tell you?"

"Her career demands so much of her time, but I asked a few times about my dad's family when I was younger. All she ever said was that I have his eyes, and that he died when I was two. I stopped asking when I got into acting as a teenager, then with the constant travels, my life stayed so busy up until now that I have come to terms with not having a father."

An actor! Quite an interesting revelation. He definitely wasn't staying in a town he considered boring.

With cold air seeping through her jumpsuit to her legs, Chloe suggested a quick stop as they approached Theda's ice cream and coffee shop. A great distraction to hide her disappointment.

"So, how long have you been acting?" she asked as they headed toward the cheerful shop.

He chuckled. "Well, I don't act anymore, that was just my childhood thing."

He explained that his TV role as a doctor had inspired him to pursue his current profession. "I travel from one third world country to another, sometimes with big organizations and sometimes with small church groups, where there's an urgent need for doctors." He added, "I come back and work for six months, so I can sponsor my next trip."

That information left her breathless. She admired him for using his gift to help those less fortunate, without even getting paid. Here she'd been judging him based on his material assets, and for being an actor who never settled in one place, yet acting had been a stepping stone for him to get to where God wanted him. "That's such a noble, respectable pursuit, Zach. What you're doing feeds the needs and satisfies your wanderlust at the same time."

"Nicely said." Zach grinned and held the door open for Chloe as they arrived at the shop.

A freckled woman in her mid-thirties stared at them with a wide grin.

"Hi, Stefanie!" Chloe greeted, and so did Zach.

He ordered hot chocolate, and Chloe ordered coffee. When Zach reached for his wallet, Chloe stepped in front of him. "I insist on paying. You're a guest."

He didn't argue.

Stefanie, the store owners' daughter, gave Chloe a questioning look. "Are you going to introduce your friend here?" She handed Zach a steaming cup, and one to Chloe.

Not that it was Stefanie's business. The woman loved spreading gossip on social media, and the ice cream shop served as gossip central, as well.

Chloe thought of a kind but concise response while she dug for money from her purse. She dropped a ten dollar bill onto the counter. "This is Zach Eron."

Stefanie's eyes widened in awe. "The grandson... related to William, the town's founder?"

"Yes." Chloe kept her response short, since she had work to do. She elbowed Zach and nudged him forward as she turned and walked towards the exit. Zach followed.

"Have a great day, Stefanie," she hollered on her way out.

"What was that all about back there?" Zach asked when they were back on the sidewalk.

"This is Eron. If you don't want yours and my picture to end up on Facebook or Instagram, just keep moving, the less words the better."

"What if I want my pictures to end up on the town's Instagram page?"

What did he just say? She stopped walking and stared at him. "Wh...why?"

He shrugged. "How many times am I caught on camera walking with a beautiful woman?"

His eyes softened and she dropped her gaze. Overwhelmed by the compliment, she almost forgot how to breathe, let alone remember how to respond. Instead she asked, "so, how long have you traveled as a doctor?"

"Seven years," he said. "If I include the three years of my residence in Australia. I worked in the Netherlands for one year, but an urgent opportunity to travel in a third world country landed on my lap and I haven't stopped traveling since then. Even though I majored in Plastics, while I'm out there, I get to do a little bit of everything." He nodded slowly, with fondness. "I'd originally planned to do this until I turned thirty, but I'm still at it, two years beyond that. I was hoping to take a break after I follow up with some patients in New Zealand in July. I want to make sure the incisions and wounds are healing properly."

He sipped his beverage and continued. "I have a job lined up in the Netherlands as soon as I come back from New Zealand. They give a high pay for plastic surgeons. God willing, I'll stay there for two years, then maybe return to whichever country God leads me next."

Chloe could only nod in agreement. She had great respect for anyone God called on a mission, and who was obedient.

Would she ever do something like that? She was content with her town, and the life she had going—if only her business picked up, then all would be well. She sipped her coffee and tightened her grip on the bag in her other hand.

"This hot chocolate is the best," Zach said, pulling her thoughts from dreamland. "The one thing I love about your town so far is the food."

"Really? How many restaurants have you visited in Eron so far?"

"Just the Italian place; Ri…"

"Ricci's." She finished for him.

"Yes, that's the name. When I came for a couple of days during Christmas time, I ate all my meals there, and then last night. I loved their soup. It had an authentic homemade taste to it," he said. "It has been a while since I ate homemade food, as you can imagine."

"When was the last time you ate a real home-cooked meal?"

He stopped walking and scratched his beard. "If it's American food, then I'm not sure, but for ethnic food, it was recent." He mentioned a home in Ireland where he and his friend had visited a year ago and had eaten dinner there. He also described a ceremony the residents had put on for the six doctors while in the Philippines as a thank you for treating them. "That was my last home-cooked meal."

"You should come to my house for dinner...I mean my parent's house." The words slipped out without thinking. In this town, everyone would do the same for him if they heard his story. "My grandma makes the best fried chicken."

He smiled from ear to ear. "I knew if I sounded pathetic, you would feel sorry for me and invite me to dinner."

"Are you telling the truth, or are you just telling the story to get yourself dinner invitations?"

He made a dramatic gesture of crossing his heart with his fingers. "That's the true pathetic story of my life." He grinned.

"Why do I get the feeling that I might regret this?" She smiled.

"Just tell me when and where, and I'll be there."

"I'll talk to my mom and grandma first, and then I will text you."

"Oh." He patted his jean pockets and pulled out his Galaxy, then handed it to her. "Just enter your number in there, and I'll text you so you can have mine. Plus it will be nice to have the phone number of a native, in case I have some questions about the town or get attacked by some residents."

Her lips willingly gave in to a soft laugh as she accepted his phone. After punching her number into his phone, she handed it back and resumed walking. "We're here." She pointed her chin to the old cement building.

Zach climbed the steps two at a time and held the door for her. The Town Hall included a library on one side, the courtrooms to the other, and straight ahead was the post office.

Once inside, they disposed of their cups in the recycle bin. Familiar faces wandered the hallway, waving at Chloe, their gazes lingering on Zach.

A couple of old ladies she knew whispered to each other before greeting them. "See you at Bingo Night tomorrow?" one of them asked, staring at Zach.

"Yes, I will be there." She went to Bingo Night often, and occasionally took her grandma, although Chloe was the youngest player in the group.

"Bring your friend, too" the golden haired one suggested shyly.

"Uh..." Chloe turned to Zach, then back to the two ladies. "He's busy and…"

"I would like to come."

Of course he did! The women giggled happily and said their goodbyes.

After sending the package, Zach became intrigued by some of the pictures that hung on the building's off-white wall. Most of them depicted Eron's history, which naturally involved Zach's family.

"This is what the town used to look like?" He pointed at the black and white picture with the town of Eron in the late 1800s.

Chloe stepped beside him. "Yes."

He studied the picture and moved to the next, until one seemed to capture his attention. "So, this is William J. Eron my…"

"Great, great… grandfather." She stared up at him before he returned his gaze to the man with a half smile in the black and white picture.

He examined another picture with more family members. "And this?"

Chloe tilted her head to study the picture. "This would be your grandma and grandpa when they were little."

After Chloe had explained all the pictures he seemed drawn to, they stepped outside to a gray, mid-morning sky.

"Best tour ever!" he said.

"You must have such terrible tours if you consider this the best," she said as they trekked down the final step. The clicking of a camera caught their attention and they turned in time to see an older woman capture their photo.

"Oh, no!" Chloe said.

"Feels like we're in Hollywood, with the aggressive paparazzi."

Chloe had no idea what a Hollywood lifestyle was like, but she could imagine the paparazzi intruding on a person's privacy. "I guess this is not new to you, since you used to be an actor."

"Not me exactly, but my mom and sister experience a lot of that, since they're still in the acting industry."

They walked side by side on Main Street as if she had no place to be, while she listened to Zach tell her about Hollywood and his childhood in the busy city.

"There you are!"

They both turned at the deep voice and stilled.

"Oh! Noah," Chloe said, feeling guilty, as if she were caught doing something wrong.

"I was looking for you," he said, ignoring Zach's presence. "I brought you an afternoon snack. I figured you could use one, since you had a busy day."

She smiled at him. "That's so thoughtful of you. Thank you."

He sighed slowly, and finally stared at Zach, or was it a glare?

"I don't know if you've met Zach yet," Chloe said.

Zach stretched out his hand and Noah hesitantly accepted it for a brief handshake, his expression hooded. "Only on Instagram. My sister texted me a screenshot of your picture at town hall." His tone held an edge to it.

Noah's teenage sister had all the time in the world. What else would teenagers do when they had phones these days?

"News sure travels fast around here." Zach scratched his beard and gave a sheepish grin.

Noah didn't seem to find that amusing. "I'll walk with you to the shop." Noah stepped between Zach and Chloe, on her right side.

Ignoring Noah's indirect message for him to step aside, Zach moved to Chloe's left side and kept his strides even with them.

This was surely a day to remember. Her body stiffened with tension as she walked with two men, one on each side.

"I believe you were born and raised here as well?" Zach directed his question at Noah, an obvious attempt to break the awkward silence.

Noah grunted his response. The silence intensified until the sound of a camera interrupted it, accompanied by a flash from the camera.

"Do you guys have a lot of paparazzi down here?" Zach asked.

"Only when you're new in town." She shrugged. "It gives people something different they can gossip about."

"Stefanie!" Noah shouted at the plump woman, who grinned at them before she lifted her cell phone towards them and disappeared back to the ice-cream shop.

"Yep, another social media shot," Chloe said. "At least Eron will have something to talk about for the next few days."

Yet somehow Chloe had a feeling that today was the beginning of many days she would be on the town's gossip page, as long as Zach was in town.

CHAPTER 4

Struggling to sleep, Zach blinked in the weak morning light that filtered through the blinds. A glance at his phone showed five thirty am.

After Zach had spoken to the realtor yesterday, she'd come to inspect the house and told him all the things he needed to clear out before listing the house for sale. He thought of the array of boxes in the basement, especially the ones that had pictures in them.

Not only had he never met his grandparents on his dad's side, Zach had never seen a single photo of his dad and that side of the family until two days ago, when Chloe had pointed them out at town hall.

Something had awakened in him since then–something that had compelled him to look around the house for more pictures of his dad's family.

Too much work to do.

Throwing the covers to the side, Zach pulled himself out of bed and marveled through the two-story stone house. It had been a shock to him, his mom and sister, too, when Zach had been contacted by the attorney and given details of his grandpa Derek's will.

He slid his fingers along the staircase railing. The old wood felt too rough underneath his fingers, and he dropped his hands to his side before he could get a splinter.

Even though he'd never been to Eron before, the scents of the old house and cinnamon seemed oddly familiar. He felt a sense of déjà vu as he studied the random framed pictures on the wall.

As he'd been warned by the attorney, one of the rooms was indeed filled to the brim with stuff, much to Zach's amazement. Everything Zach owned could fit in his car. Being constantly on the move, accumulation was not an option.

He assumed all the things would have to go before he could sell the house, but he didn't know where to start. His mother probably wouldn't want any of the items, since they were not her style.

Starting with the smaller boxes, Zach lifted one off the pile and tugged the flaps open. He sneezed when dust tickled his nose. The sight of a stack of photos in Ziploc bags unexpectedly snagged him by the throat.

Flipping through the pictures, he noticed some were frail and yellowed, an indication they'd been taken years ago. He continued paging through his grandparents' entire life, enthralled in a way he hadn't expected.

He slowed at the familiar face of his mom, a younger Monique standing next to a green-eyed man, who stared at her with longing. Zach's heart stopped for a few seconds as he studied the picture of his mom and dad a lot longer than he'd intended to. He had a past beyond California, and flipping through it made him feel good and sad for all he didn't know.

He felt the urge to call and share with his mom, but she was probably busy filming in a movie somewhere, and the last thing she would want to chat about would be her past.

A part of him felt glad he came, especially that he'd met Chloe. Speaking of whom, her warm eyes the color of milk chocolate, came to mind. He hadn't missed the disappointment in her face when he'd mentioned his plans to sell the house.

Why she cared about the house, he had no idea, but all Zach knew was that spending time with her as they strolled along the quiet street the day before, and the next evening when he'd joined her to play bingo with the rowdy and fun group of elderly people, had felt refreshing.

The bright light streaming through the curtains reminded Zach of Leticia's invitation to her house for breakfast at nine. Putting the pictures back in the box, Zach closed the flaps and set it aside.

After taking a shower, he drove to his neighbor's house. The pink Victorian home came into view. Thankful for the clear sky, he had a feeling that it was going to be a beautiful day as he stepped out of the beige rented Land Rover.

An hour later, Zach leaned back, fork in hand, with the scent of bacon, cinnamon and maple syrup wafting through the air. He lifted the fork to his mouth and devoured another piece of french toast, letting the syrup melt in his mouth.

When Leticia had called last night, she'd asked about Zach's trip and experiences, and listened to every detail. She'd insisted he join her and her husband for breakfast. Not wanting to settle for cereal over a home-cooked breakfast, Zach had agreed.

The petite woman lifted another piece of toast with the tongs and slid it onto his plate.

Zach patted his stomach. "I'm so stuffed." Two untouched strips of bacon remained on his plate, and he had no idea where to put them.

"That's why I have the belly to show for it." Leticia's husband, Garth, patted his own round stomach. "Between Letty's cooking and baked goods from patients, couldn't avoid the temptation."

Leticia settled back in her chair. "Help yourself to more juice, Zach."

Forgetting about the sugar content, Zach tilted the pitcher to fill his glass halfway with the orange liquid. "Thank you, Leticia."

Garth shared about his job as the town's doctor and its challenges, like the late night he'd had last night when he'd gone to help deliver a colt.

"You're a vet, too?" Zach asked.

Garth let out a low laugh. "In Eron, a doctor gets to do everything, fills in all the gaps of what any doctor would do." He talked about the first time he'd birthed a cow, trying to use his knowledge from humans. "Nice to have today and tomorrow off. I only get a few days off whenever a doctor from Colorado Springs comes to Eron a couple of times a month."

Garth dropped a ladleful of syrup onto his toast, which was already swimming in maple. "You sure remind me of your grandpa. The way you talk." He then offered the serving plate of sausages to Zach, despite his objection about being full.

Zach shook his head.

"And those green eyes, too." Leticia peered at Zach. "Your dad had the same eyes, just as your grandpa Derek did."

"It's interesting that you're a doctor, too, just like your grandpa. He founded our hospital, you know." Garth's pale eyes twinkled under bushy gray brows. "Looks like it runs in the family." He began naming all the doctors that had been in Zach's family, starting with the town's founder, to Zach's dad, who had been a military doctor.

While at the town hall, the notes underneath William Eron's picture mentioned him being a physician who was passing through the land, along with farmers who'd developed a friendship during their journey. They'd settled in this area due to an abundant water supply from streams and green pastures for their animals, and the town of Eron had been established.

"We never got to talk about your trip to Love's Boutique when I called you last night." He blinked from his thoughts when the old woman changed the subject as she moved to the kitchen and returned with a glass carafe with dark liquid, then tilted it to Zach's cup. He liked his coffee black. "What did you think of the town, especially the store owner, Chloe?"

Zach nodded, since his mouth was stuffed with the last piece of bread. Memories of his walk with her brought warmth. It had felt amazing, as if he was meant to know her, like they belonged together. For once he'd allowed himself to dwell on that thought, until her boyfriend showed up and staked his claim by stepping between them. Noah had acted like he was about to toss Zach over a nearby cliff.

He could handle being tossed over, but the way Chloe's eyes lit up when the guy talked to her had taken all Zach's acting skills to mask the disappointment he felt at the time.

No, he shouldn't feel bothered at all, because he was leaving. The fork clanked on his plate when he set it down, and he straightened. "Yes, I met the girls at her shop, too. In fact, my realtor's office is there."

He decided not to mention Bingo Night that Leticia did not attend. It was much safer to talk about the realtor than anything that involved Chloe, to remind himself that his residency in town was temporary.

The lady was staring at him as if waiting for him to give her all the details of his time on Main Street.

"I guess you know Chloe, then?" *What happened to keeping Chloe out of this conversation?*

Leticia's gray brows stretched out as she smiled fondly. Of course she knew her, everybody knew everyone in the tiny town. He was the outsider who was becoming more popular by the minute on the town's Instagram page.

He'd checked it out that afternoon after Chloe's boyfriend mentioned he was on the page. He smiled at what they'd called him. ***"Cute guy with Chloe Love? Noah hangs in the balance,"*** the headline had said.

"Chloe comes to my house often." Leticia jolted him out of his thoughts. "In fact she cleaned your house."

His lips parted in surprise. "I will have to get the bill from her so I can pay for her time and services." *Another excuse to see her.*

Waving his offer away with her hand, Leticia took the coffee pot back to the counter before rejoining them at the table. "She will not accept your money. Your grandparents meant a lot to her and her family." Leticia folded her hands on the table. "I asked her to find someone to do the cleaning but she said she wanted to do it by herself."

Zach's eyes opened wide in wonder. "Did she buy all the baskets of snacks too?"

"Everything, and she didn't give me any receipts, so I don't have a bill for you."

Zach thought about the new bedding, the comforter with the clean detergent smell, the new towels on the bathroom rack, the rug in the living room and the candles throughout the house that created a sweet aroma. "I have to pay her. She spent a lot of money."

"Good luck with that, my darling," said Leticia, her accent evident. Zach had learned that she was from Macedonia, and had met Garth on a tour bus. "She will never accept payment, especially if she finds out that you're Derek's grandson."

She'd already learned that when Zach had introduced himself.

The conversation moved to everyday things. With excitement sparkling in his eyes, Garth talked about his horse back riding adventures. "In ten days, Dr. Comic is coming to relieve me at the hospital for four days, and I'm going horseback riding with my buddy."

"Isn't it too snowy to ride horses?" Zach knew nothing about horses, since he'd never ridden one before, but he thought such things were done in the summer.

Garth scratched his gray beard. "Snow should melt in a couple of days, and the forecast shows clear skies by then."

"While you're here..." Leticia changed the subject, staring at Zach. "I want you to join us for dinner every evening, so that you don't have to trouble with cooking for yourself."

He had no intention of cooking when they made such good food in town.

"Chloe invited me to dinner at their house on Wednesday." He wished it was tomorrow, instead of three days away.

"She's a sweetie, she's so good to everyone in town."

Everyone. He felt a slight pang at the thought of her inviting anyone else. Zach hoped that she'd invited him because she wanted to get to know him more, just as he wanted to know her and spend more time with her even though he was only in town for a short period of time.

Chloe studied her reflection in the full-length mirror in her bedroom and tucked loose strands of her dark hair behind her ears for the fifth time. After washing her hair, she'd blow-dried and curled it into bouncy waves with a curling iron.

She pursed her lips to make sure the lip-gloss was evenly spread, then reached for her phone from the dresser to check it for the fourth time, just in case Zach had texted to change his mind about dinner, or wanting better directions. She only saw the earlier texts he'd sent. One at five am, saying he was looking forward to dinner, and another one at ten asking if he needed to bring anything.

The time showed four thirty, which meant he would be arriving in thirty minutes. Chloe felt warm and giddy all of a sudden. Letting out a slow breath, she stepped out of her room to go straighten the house one more time.

She could only hope that her mom's attitude about having Zach join them for dinner had changed. Upon Chloe telling her she'd invited him, Cynthia, never one to turn down guests, had been hesitant.

"It's just that the new guy with you on social media shouldn't be here. He's a threat to your relationship with Noah," she'd said.

Her grandma, Jeanie, was in favor of Zach coming. She'd been a close friend to his grandma, Lydia. Plus, Chloe's grandma was doing most of the cooking anyway.

Chloe's dad sat in the fabric recliner in the living-room, the Eron Tribune in hand, eyes intent on the page. "Hi, Dad."

He took his eyes off the local paper and greeted Chloe. "Hi, honey."

He smiled mischievously and returned his full attention to the paper in his hand. Chloe assumed he was staring at the picture of her strolling the street with two men. She'd seen the headline earlier, "***Love in the Balance.***" *Eron's grandson, with local golden girl Chloe Love? Where does that leave Noah Buzz?*

She moved to the dining table to re-adjust the center piece she had set earlier and squeezed between the extra stools set in between the chairs to straighten the table. She moved around the house, lighting the candles that she'd set out earlier, a few on the window sills, and some by the entrance table.

Jeanie whipped mashed potatoes in the pan, while Cynthia sat in her wheelchair stirring something on the stove. The stove and several cabinets had been redesigned at a lower level to give Cynthia access to the kitchen when she needed it.

Cynthia lifted a wooden spoon and blew on it. With her hand, she grabbed a piece of something and popped it in her mouth, no doubt her okra, since it was the one thing she insisted on cooking whenever they had guests. Unfortunately, nobody was bold enough to tell her it tasted awful.

The smell of fried chicken and comfort food hung in the air. Chloe sauntered to the kitchen. "Why do we have three extra stools added to the chairs?"

Cynthia turned at Chloe's voice. Rubbing her hands on her apron, she smiled. "I invited Noah and his family over." She then gave Chloe a once over. "Noah will like that sweater you're wearing by the way. Green always looks nice on you."

She turned her attention back to the contents in her pan as the words registered in Chloe's mind. "Did you just say that you invited Noah?" Cynthia nodded and Chloe's blood heated with discomfort. "Why didn't you tell me that he was coming?"

Cynthia spoke dismissively, not looking up from her pan. "Well, I figured I could make a whole evening out by inviting our special friends, but only Noah and his mom will make it."

"Your ma thought the more the merrier," Grandma clarified.

Chloe enjoyed Noah's company, and she should be happy, but she knew her mom had an agenda. Her mood affected, she wondered how things would go with the two guys sitting across the table from each other since they'd gotten off on the wrong foot.

When the doorbell rang, Chloe's heart stilled. Was it Noah or Zach at the door? Her hands flew to her hair, shoving a wild stubborn curl back in place. Her heart raced as she turned the door knob.

She hoped the disappointment didn't show on her face when Noah's mom greeted her.

"Thanks for inviting us," Millie said. Noah's smile reached his eyes, a bouquet of mixed roses in his hand and a box in the other. The sun had already set, but the fading glow promised another hour of daylight.

"It's always nice to see you guys." *Except today.* Chloe smiled, though not the most genuine smile.

"These are for Mom and Grandma." Noah handed Chloe the flowers, then smiled as he offered her a box of chocolates. "These are for you."

He called Cynthia 'Mom,' which would make things even more awkward should their relationship fail to make it. Chloe's family was getting more attached to Noah each passing day.

Taking the flowers and chocolates from him, Chloe stood on tiptoe and planted a kiss on his cheek. "Thank you, Noah."

While Millie and Noah hung their coats on the rack, Chloe took the flowers to the kitchen. Cynthia lit up when she sniffed the roses. Chloe hoped her mother's smile would hold up through the entire evening.

CHAPTER 5

Zach's tires sloshed through the wet snow. He would need a car wash, but it would have to wait till tomorrow since it would be late by the time he left Chloe's place—her parent's place.

He'd had plenty of time to get himself ready, given the fact that he'd been up since four am. That had nothing to do with this invitation, of course. At least he could blame it on the time change instead.

He scratched his jaw, which he'd spent almost an hour grooming to sport a simple stubble beard. He'd given himself a haircut, too, since he wasn't up to bouncing around the town in search of a barber.

The drive was peaceful. The sun that had offered its warmth earlier in the day had slipped behind the highest peak. With almost an hour left of daylight, Zach could see several homes poking through the trees. Mostly log cabins, and a few brick homes that seemed closer to each other than the houses where his own property was located.

Using Chloe's directions, he was reminded to keep an eye out for a red and white house, since it was next to her parents' house. After passing several properties with split rail fences, he approached the red and white house with a red barn. Zach rolled down the window and the smell of horse manure filled the cab.

When a ranch house came into view, his emotions were a mix of anxiety and excitement. His stomach gave a weird growl and he regretted eating a handful of candied nuts instead of lunch. He hoped the rumbling was because of the nervousness.

He'd never sat with parents before, not parents of… what was Chloe to him? A friend, he guessed her to be.

Gravel crunched underneath his tires when he parked his Land Rover in the driveway. He slammed the door closed behind him and took a moment to study the tan house and the long ramp that led from the sidewalk onto the porch. He climbed the few stairs, instead, to reach the front door. Raising his knuckles, he rapped on the sturdy oak door.

The chatter of voices and laughter coming from the house indicated a bigger gathering than he'd anticipated. He smoothed his dark jacket one more time. His stomach rumbled again just as the door swung open.

Chloe's genuine smile was all he needed for his tense muscles to relax.

"Zach." She stared at him breathlessly, and Zach felt the urge to bend and give her a hug in greeting, but she gestured him inside. "It's good to see you again."

His eyes lingered over the wrap sweater that curved around her slender waist. No doubt she'd designed it, since the seniors at bingo night had raved about her designing all her clothes. "You as well. Thanks for the invite."

The chatter died down when he walked into the hallway, and every eye in the dining room pinned on him. He also noticed that he was the only person present with fair skin.

Moses? Or was his name Noah? Chloe hadn't told him that her boyfriend would be here. *Well, that figures.*

As Chloe took the coat from him, their hands brushed, and he whispered for her ears alone, "Why do I get the feeling that I'm going to end up on the menu?"

She winced at him. "I'm sorry, my mom decided to invite more people. But everything's going to be okay," she assured him in a whisper.

So it hadn't been her idea to invite her boyfriend.

All eyes were still fixed on him as he stepped into the dining room.

"Come join us!" A dark skinned man whom Zach guessed to be Chloe's dad beckoned him to the table, warmth radiating from his face.

After Chloe had made introductions, Zach extended a hand to Cynthia, who was deposited in a wheelchair. The woman hesitated before accepting his hand for a brief handshake.

Zach then shook George's hand, and Chloe's grandma Jeanie's. Jeanie smiled cheerfully at him underneath salt and pepper hair that was cropped short.

After handshakes all around, Cynthia pointed to a chair next to Chloe's dad, where she ordered him to sit. Chloe sat next to her mom, across from Zach. The rectangular table was long but narrow. His feet touched Chloe's, and her chair scraped the floor when she scooted it back. Jeanie excused herself and Chloe followed her to the kitchen.

Zach had never felt intimidated in his entire life as he felt right now under Cynthia's watchful eyes. Neither Noah nor his mom said anything to him. Chloe's dad was silent but his mind seemed far from the table. Should he bolt and call it an evening?

Jeanie returned and placed a hot pad in the center of the table, and Chloe hauled in a pan of golden fried chicken. After setting the fragrant pan on the hot pad, Chloe left for the kitchen again.

Zach pushed back his chair. He would rather help than stare at the stern faces.

"I'll help." He took a bowl of steaming mashed potatoes from Chloe and waited for her to grab another bowl of vegetables. Her grandma carried two more bowls and carefully placed them on the table before they sat.

Cynthia cleared her throat. "Will you say grace for us, Zach?"

He'd never been commanded to pray, and he was not about to start today.

When he met Chloe's apologetic eyes across the table and noticed the tension in her shoulders, Zach hoped that God would understand if he just said a short, simple prayer.

"I'll…"

"I'll do it." He interrupted Chloe and dipped his chin to pray. After praying, he tilted a glass of ice cold water to his lips and set it back down. He stretched his leg underneath the table, intending to kick Chloe for assurance, except…it wasn't Chloe who was staring at him.

Uh oh. His gaze collided with Cynthia's glare, which was much colder than the iced water in his glass. Zach winced.

"Keep your feet to yourself," Cynthia snapped.

Zach felt heat creep up the back of his neck.

"Help yourself to some chicken." Jeanie handed him the bowl. Though his appetite was gone, Zach lifted the tongs and grabbed a drum stick that he placed on his plate.

The chatter resumed when Cynthia asked about Noah's current projects.

"I finally finished building Marion's guardrail fence." Noah spoke of all the people he was helping in the community and Cynthia mentioned how Noah had done all the major improvements to their house to meet Cynthia's handicapped needs.

The guy was apparently like family to them.

"That's wonderful, Noah," Zach said sincerely. "I bet you're very busy, being the town's only contractor, yet still doing volunteer projects for people."

Noah was silent as he chewed his food. He took a sip of his water before he leaned back and responded. "There's always work to do in Eron, but I have a decent crew of guys who help me out."

Noah chatted easily about his work, responding to Cynthia's and George's questions.

When the silence resumed, Jeanie passed the bowl of mashed potatoes to Zach and said, "Chloe says you travel all over the world, treating people in places with no doctors. I think that's amazing."

She was exaggerating, but Zach appreciated her attempt to include him in the conversation.

"I do. It blesses me to see the joy on people's faces when they recover from tumors and facial defects." He talked about his two friends, Rahul, the ophthalmologic doctor who specialized in vision care, and Henry, the dentist he traveled with most of the time.

Chloe and Jeanie peppered him with questions about the ups and downs in different regions, and their genuine interest encouraged Zach to share a language barrier story from his recent trip to the Philippines.

"The people put on a celebration after their family members and friends were healed. They invited us for the ceremony, with lots of food and dancing. One man walks to us and

stares at our glasses, before he asked Henry in Filipino, *Tubig?*
Henry was insulted because he was always self conscious about his
weight. He lost it. 'What? Are you saying that I'm fat?'"

Jeanie was already chuckling, George leaned forward,
eager to hear the punch line, and Chloe's eyes were bright as a
wide smile turned up her lips. The attention from everyone was
now positive, and Zach relaxed.

"Thankfully, I knew a few words in Tagalog, and that's one
I had read in the dictionary before the trip. I had to save the man
from Henry's rage and explained to Henry that *tubig* means
water."

Millie laughed until her eyes watered. Even Cynthia almost
managed a smile. Zach joined in the laughter as the memories of
that celebration surfaced in his mind. When the laughter subsided,
some people sipped their drinks, while others scooped seconds of
food.

Zach bit into his drumstick. He'd chosen to eat sparingly
because his stomach felt unsettled.

"You should try some okra," Cynthia urged, handing him a
bowl of green stuff. "I made it."

Zach had always avoided certain vegetables, and okra was
one of them. Since this was Cynthia's first genuine sentence to
him, he had to try it, especially since everyone else had some on
their plates.

His brows furrowed the moment the slimy taste hit his
tongue. The scent was already making him nauseous. There was no
way he could swallow it.

"What do you think of the okra?" Cynthia asked.

His mouth still full of vegetables, Zach attempted a tactful response. He reached for his napkin and spit the vile stuff into it, then wrapped it instantly. "I'm sorry. Okra is just...I know yours tastes good, but it's just... a texture thing."

"Everybody likes my okra," Cynthia said defensively.

How could he tell her that it tasted awful, not because of the way she cooked it but because it was one of the few vegetables he couldn't stand the taste of? Seemed he'd just made an enemy for life. His stomach made a gurgling sound.

Uh oh. He really needed to make a trip to the bathroom. He pushed his chair back and stared pleadingly at Chloe. "Can I talk to you, please?"

Chloe walked with him to the kitchen, and he could feel himself finally breathe. "I'm sorry about the…"

"You don't have to apologize," she whispered.

"Where's your trash? He held out the napkin, and Chloe opened the cabinet underneath the sink where the trash can was kept.

"I need to use the bathroom really bad." He spoke in a whisper, since he could feel the watchful eyes from the table on him.

"You okay?" Chloe's face expressed genuine concern.

He placed a hand to his stomach. "I think I ate too many nuts earlier."

"To the right." She quickly pointed to a hallway near the entrance.

As if he hadn't made a bad enough impressions for the day, the toilet wouldn't flush when he pushed the handle. He searched the cabinet under the sink for a plunger, but came up with nothing.

Great. So great!

God sure knew how to humble someone, and today was apparently Zach's moment of humility. He stood in the hallway and waited for Chloe to spot him. When she finally looked up and saw him, she walked his way.

"Do you...uh...have a toilet plunger?" he asked. *Seriously, Zach, what a way to make a first impression on a girl!*

When Zach finally made his way back to the table, an awkward silence settled, broken only by the clattering of forks on plates. Zach stared at his half-eaten food with no intention of taking another bite.

Mercifully, the meal ended before he could disgrace himself further. After Zach and Chloe cleared the table and loaded dishes into the dishwasher, they sat down.

Jeanie asked, "Have you been able to go through some of your grandparents things?"

That's what he would've been doing earlier before coming here, but he'd been too consumed with the dinner invitation to think of anything else but how the evening with Chloe's family would turn out.

"A little bit," he said. "After Chloe showed me some pictures of my family at the town hall the other day, I found myself intrigued and went back home and browsed through more pictures."

"Did you find any pictures of yourself when you were young?" Jeanie asked.

Why would his pictures be in Eron? "I saw a picture of my mom and dad."

"Good!" Jeanie said. "There should be some pictures of you somewhere in the house. Your mom brought you to stay with your grandparents for two summers." The old woman's face wrinkled. "I think you were six and seven years old. You stayed for no longer than two weeks each summer."

His mom had never told him such details either. Did Chloe know about this? He arched a brow at her, but her eyes didn't give anything away.

Zach was about to ask for more details when George winced as if in pain, and one of his hands flew to his back. Chloe stared at George with concern.

Zach's attention shifted to the man instead. "Are you okay?"

"I'm okay." George took rapid breaths. "It's just… the pain comes and goes. I might need my medicine."

Chloe instantly pushed a chair back and returned with pills.

In the short time she was gone, Zach was told about the man's back pain that had lasted for two years. He also learned that

George's x-rays, taken a year ago, didn't show anything of concern. George was content with the medicine that used to dull the pain, but now he depended on it more often than not.

"We need to look at it soon." Knowing how busy the town's doctor was, Zach assumed it might be a while before Garth could do something about George's back. "Let's get you to the hospital for an MRI."

"I don't know if that will show anything, but Dr. Garth hasn't recommended it yet."

"Ready for dessert?" Jeanie's cheery voice interrupted them as she left the table and returned with a pie that she deposited on the table.

"Pecan Pie," Cynthia said. "It's Noah's favorite." She smiled at Noah, then turned to Zach with a defiant glare. "Noah does so much for our family, we have to take special care of him."

If the lady was trying to make a point, she was doing a decent job. Noah tugged at the collar of his polo shirt, appearing uncomfortable with Cynthia's compliments.

Chloe pushed back her chair, and dropped a napkin on the table. "You know what, Mom? Zach and I need to get going. I had promised to take him to the cake shop for dessert."

She gave Noah an apologetic smile, with a promise to see him on Valentine's Day, then said goodbye to Noah's mom before she strode to the door. After sliding on her coat, she pulled Zach's coat from the rack.

They hadn't talked about going to the cake shop, but relief flooded through Zach, since he was done with Cynthia's coldness.

He thanked Cynthia and Jeanie for dinner, then scheduled to call George tomorrow as soon as he sought Garth's permission for an MRI. He hoped for tomorrow.

He gave Noah and his mom a curt nod before joining Chloe at the door. If having a bad experience earned him Chloe for the evening, then well, dessert at the cake shop, indeed!

"You can follow me, I'll go get my car from the garage," Chloe suggested.

"Let me drive you, I can bring you back."

"You're sure?"

He didn't plan on going back into the house. "I'm sure." He also didn't need any dessert, but he was not passing up the opportunity to spend time with her.

Twenty minutes later, they sat in a cafe, Chloe enjoying her cheesecake while Zach gulped down the chamomile tea she'd suggested. What he wouldn't give to have a piece of cheesecake, but his stomach had resigned for the day.

She apologized for what seemed like the tenth time. He'd lost track.

"If being rejected by your mom gives me this kind of day, then it's worth it. When should I come again for dinner?" he playfully asked.

She chuckled, showcasing the whitest teeth he'd ever seen.

"My mother is not as bad as she acted tonight. She can be bossy at times, but it's because she's catching up to parenting. She used to be a wild child, had me at sixteen, and left me with grandma to be raised." Her smile faded. "She returned in a wheelchair after a horrific accident and years in therapy. That's how she met George, while in therapy." She moved the fork through her cake. "She's not the easiest person, but I'm trying to adapt from years of wondering why she left me, to now experiencing what it's like to have a mother."

Zach's chest tightened with grief over what had happened to Cynthia, and what Chloe had been through growing up without either one of her parents. "I'm so sorry, Chloe."

She shrugged, "Could have been worse I guess. I'm glad I have my mother back."

"George is not your real father?"

"Nope, but he's so patient with my mom, and very good to me and my grandma. Since I have no father, and George has no kids, I decided to call him Dad. Feels good calling someone Dad."

Zach understood. Even if he didn't have anyone to call Dad, he had a heavenly Father. "Yes, it feels good."

"How about your grandpa?" he asked. "What happened to him?"

"My grandfather died before I was born."

After hearing her story, Zach better not whine about his life, because he had his mom and sister, and his grandparents from Monique's side of the family.

As if sensing his thoughts, she said, "I had a good life. Lots of kids in my situation end up in foster care, but God has really been good to me, so I can't complain."

Zach nodded slowly, taking in Chloe's words of gratitude. She'd given up her career in Boston and returned home to take care of her family. "I will try my best to do some research so I can help George get that pain under control. He can't keep taking all those pills–pretty soon they will give him major side effects."

"Thank you."

To shift the conversation to something lighter, he asked, "What made you go into fashion?"

"I always had a passion for it. I used to do sewing and quilting club with my grandma."

It turned out she had been in the same group as Zach's grandma Lydia, and Zach felt more intrigued than ever by Chloe. She was his ticket to knowing his dad's side of the family.

Remembering she'd mentioned a charity project, he asked, "How are the arrangements going for that fashion show? Is there any way I can help you out with that?"

"I'm still not sure that I will get the right audience, but Jules is working hard to send out promos on social media."

"I can help spread the word for you," he offered.

She looked doubtful, and Zach explained, "I have lots of friends in LA who love to hear about new designers, plus my mom and sister love new fashions, and they have friends too." He said, "If I add that to the friends that I still have in Hollywood, they can ignite a media firestorm with one phone call."

She stared at him, speechless, then she let out a sigh of relief. "That would be wonderful! I just hope my designs will be good enough for your Hollywood friends."

He narrowed his gaze on her. "If the clothes I've seen you wear are part of your designs, then you have nothing to worry about."

She smiled and bit her lower lip before she spoke. "I have a suit in mind, an idea I thought... you would be the perfect model for it."

He leaned forward. "Is that so?"

"You have the right physique, then add in your endearing personality, and we're good to go." The words were coming out of her mouth so fast, perhaps she was nervous. "Any chance I can take your measurements for you to model it?"

He'd posed for the camera several times and knew the ins and outs of modeling, but he liked the idea of teasing her. "Me? Modeling?"

"Yeah, you have the perfect appearance, fit and walk, and now that your beard is gone..."

"Are you flirting with me, Chloe Love?"

She fiddled with her fork, embarrassed. "Uh...forget it!" She stared back at her plate.

"I'll do it."

Her head lifted, soft brown eyes found his, and in a voice that was barely a whisper, she asked, "You will?"

Zach nodded. "Sure. Just tell me when and where."

After Chloe thanked him several times, they chatted about other topics. Zach felt relaxed in Chloe's warm presence, and a feeling of familiarity and comfort washed over him.

"How are the house projects going?" she asked before she dipped her fork for the final piece of her cheesecake.

"Good." Zach sipped the now cold tea. "I still have much more work to do than I expected. I probably need to hire someone to do some drywall."

"If you need quality work done, Noah is your man."

Did it have to be him? "Anyone else? Afraid he might tie me up on a tree."

"He wouldn't do that. He's a very nice person." She smiled and stared at the glass window. "My family couldn't have made it without his help." In other words, whatever Zach was plotting about Chloe, he'd better shove it to the side. "And I'm afraid to say that he's your only choice for that kind of work."

Pretending not to be affected by her fondness of Noah, he groaned. "Okay."

"I will ask him for you."

He selfishly didn't want to give them a reason to go on another date on his account. "I would rather ask him myself, if you can give me his number."

"I'll text it to you."

Much later that night, as he gave in to the pull of sleep, images fluttered through Zach's mind. He kept seeing Chloe and her beautiful smile. Anyone with the last name 'Love' had to have a special kind of love and a unique smile.

"Chloe." He rolled onto his side in the soft rickety bed. "I know you have a boyfriend, and I'm only here for a limited time."

Despite all the obstacles that should keep him from thinking about the dark skinned beauty, Zach couldn't hold back the feeling that he was going to get to know Chloe Love on a deeper level.

CHAPTER 6

Two days later, Zach sat in Eron's Recreation Center gym for their Valentine's Day dance, an event Chloe had organized earlier this year as another way to raise money for the Senior Assisted Living facility. Zach had generously volunteered to run the raffle booth.

Before coming to the dance, Zach had been able to get George, Chloe's dad, to the hospital to have an MRI taken of his back. With Dr. Garth's approval, Zach had left his own information with the radiology department so they could send the results to him.

"I'll take a raffle ticket, please." A woman with caramel hair pulled him from his thoughts.

Zach placed his hand in the jar and pulled out a single ticket. "This is the last one." He handed it to the woman.

"I could have used two, but, oh well." She handed him a twenty dollar bill, which was the exact price of each ticket. "I hope I can win something."

When Chloe had told him about the dance, she'd also mentioned that Noah had asked her to be his date. Zach's coming tonight was all about him wanting to support Chloe's efforts, and not him wanting to spend the afternoon with her.

Yeah, right.

Now that the raffle tickets were sold out, he leaned back in a folding chair and surveyed the room, which was crowded with ladies dressed mostly in evening and cocktail dresses, and men mostly in button down shirts. Even though it was a senior event, he was surprised to see a variety of ages had come out to show their support. Young and old couples all swayed to the tune.

"There's lots of young ladies without a date who seem to be admiring you. Why don't you ask one of them to dance?"

Zach startled and blinked at an old woman leaning towards him. He shook his head. "I'm good. Thanks."

The woman he wanted to dance with was across the room dancing with another man who hadn't left her presence since the dance floor opened twenty minutes ago.

Chloe's eyes sparkled under the dim lights, her long hair falling in waves past her shoulders. The flared cocktail dress swayed when she danced to a fast song. Purple, the color of royalty. She looked beautiful, and Zach had a hard time watching anybody else but her.

Her eyes found his and she smiled, then waved at him.

Zach contemplated stepping onto the dance floor to claim a dance. The only thing that stopped him was that deep down, he knew that Chloe was Noah's date, and she looked comfortable in the other man's arms as she twirled.

There was a force only Chloe brought out in Zach that he couldn't explain. He pushed back his chair in agitation the moment Chloe smiled at something Noah said. That must be the explanation–he wanted to be the one making her laugh.

The phone vibrated from his jeans pocket and he pulled it out. Zach gritted his teeth when his sister Addie's name displayed on the screen. She couldn't have chosen a worse time to call. With a sigh, he swiped his thumb across the screen to take his sister's call.

"Hey, Addie." Stepping away from the noise of the party, he added, "Addie, I'm gonna have to call you…"

"Don't hang up," she interrupted. "I'm at your place. Where are you?"

"My place?" He didn't really have a place in LA, since he normally leased only when he returned for a while. "What do you mean?"

"I'm right here in your little town. Can you get over here, already?"

At his grandparents' house? Zach ran a hand through his hair and tightened a fist. "It's Valentine's Day. Shouldn't you be…?"

He held his tongue and hung up. He would be glad to see his sister, and besides, Chloe was not his, and most certainly not this Valentine's Day.

The gym had been transformed into a romantic wonderland, with white lights strung across the room and candles flickering in the center of each table. The dance floor had been dismantled and replaced by elegant tables for dinner time. Soft music continued in the background.

Depending on what price ticket people had purchased, they could choose from several tables that had been set up. Some had a setting for two, while others were arranged for families or larger groups who had purchased the Valentine's Day Package. Noah had bought a table for two.

Chloe stared at Noah, who looked handsome in his dark-red, button up shirt. "I'd forgotten what a great dancer you are."

He smiled. "And how would you have known that?" He reached for a glass of iced water from the table.

Chloe fanned herself, needing to cool down from all the dancing. She was ready for another refill, but decided to wait for their server to return.

Noah was a year older than Chloe, but had graduated the same year. "First junior high dance, I sat at the bench with a few of my friends and we watched all the good dancers. My friends and I agreed that you were the best dancer on the floor."

"I'd have loved to dance with you."

She grimaced. "You didn't know I even existed."

"I knew that you existed. Not only did you grow up next door to me, but at school you were that kid who was always leading a book club or a history club, and instead of going out to movies on weekends, you preferred hanging out at the library, or with the elderly doing your sewing."

He leaned forward. "That's how well I knew you—enough to know that you wouldn't have gone out with me anyway. You always hung out with kids who were responsible and stayed out of trouble, kids the complete opposite of me. In other words, you were out of my league."

"I don't think I was out of your league."

He laughed, revealing a nice smile that crinkled his nose. "I was always drawn to the wild crowd back then and I was a fool to have not joined one of your book clubs." He reached across the table and touched the back of her hand. "Glad I'm not too late in the game."

"Yeah. Me, too," she whispered, feeling guilty for her response, since her mind kept roaming to the doctor she'd just met a few days ago. What was Zach doing right now?

Noah's steak arrived, along with Chloe's Chicken Marsala. The food smelled wonderful. She'd made the right decision in hiring two different restaurants to cater the occasion.

She prayed over their food and they dug in. While Noah talked about the addition to his house, Chloe tried not to wonder why Zach had left abruptly in the middle of the dance. She'd seen him go outside to take a call, and he'd never returned to the building. Had he received an offer for the house? Sofia, his realtor, hadn't mentioned anything to Chloe yet.

"Chloe?"

She blinked back to the present. "Uh...yeah?"

"I was asking what color would be perfect for the sun room?"

She finally poked the fork into her uneaten pasta. "I think something colorful. Green maybe, but I know you prefer..." *What did he prefer?* "Maybe a masculine color?"

"I want something you would like, too."

He was already planning their future together. How long would she have to wait until her heart felt the desire for a future with Noah? She reached for her water and took a couple of sips so she wouldn't have to respond, and was thankful when Noah switched the topic.

"Anyway, how's the fashion show preparation going?" Noah cut into his steak with a knife and forked it to his mouth.

"It's going well so far."

"What would you like me to do?" he offered.

"Maybe model a summer outfit?"

His amused expression showed he didn't think she was serious. "You're not kidding, are you?"

"I need three male models, and Zach is the only volunteer I have so far."

His face turned flat, and Chloe kicked herself. *Why did she have to bring up Zach?*

"You should be careful around him," he warned.

Chloe blinked, confused by Noah's statement.

"I can tell he likes you, and I don't know if I should be worried or not." He scooped up a bit of broccoli and put it into his mouth.

"What makes you think he likes me?"

He snorted. "The way he kept staring at you at dinner the other day at your parent's house was a test of my patience and self-control that I would rather not have to face again."

Noah wasn't the violent type, but perhaps he'd experienced a bit of jealousy, since she'd noticed the slight tension in his jaw when he'd seen Zach whispering to her the moment he'd arrived.

Chloe shrugged a shoulder. "Maybe he was staring at me to avoid colliding with mom's glare."

He cleared his throat. "Just thought I'd say what I observed."

"He's leaving." She swirled her fork through the pasta. "You don't have to worry about me falling for him." Even as she said the words, shame filled her heart for the half-truth. She needed to control the warm and giddy feeling she felt in Zach's presence, but had no idea how.

It was an hour later when Noah dropped her off at her house. Being a senior event, the dance had started at one pm and ended at three, so the seniors could be home in time for their medicine and evening news, or whatever else seniors did.

Standing on Chloe's porch, Noah inched closer. "I had a nice time."

Her heart raced, aware of what was about to happen. Would this be their first kiss?

"Me, too. Thanks for the flowers." He'd had them delivered at her place of work earlier.

Noah stared at her lips intently. No doubt her parents were busy inside, but a kiss would tie her to a relationship she wasn't ready to be committed to. She abruptly turned and reached for the door knob. "Good night, Noah."

It was several hours before bed time, she realized when she glanced at the light sky. She walked back and stood on tiptoe to give him a peck on the cheek before turning again to open the door. She waved at him. "Have a good evening."

Thankfully, her mom and dad were immersed in the TV in the living room when she strode past. On her way down the hall to her bedroom, Chloe glanced through a wide open door to see Jeanie busily spinning the sewing machine.

Chloe leaned against the door jamb and stared at the shelves that held mounds of books and magazines she read for inspiration and to keep up with design trends. She inhaled the smell of fabric and Grandma and felt a warm familiarity. This was just the same smell she'd grown up with, or at least Grandma's scent of lavender and cinnamon.

Their original house had been lost in a fire years ago. Thankfully, neither Jeanie nor Chloe had been home when the electrical fire started, but all their belongings had been lost. They'd had to move in with Derek and Lydia until they'd rebuilt their house.

After moving into the new home they'd built on the same property, she and Jeanie had designated the biggest room in the house for their sewing projects.

The moment Chloe had made the decision to move back to Eron, Jeanie had agreed to help her sew her designs. Not only did Chloe draw out the designs, but she sewed them herself when time allowed. Once, she'd had an order for a line of wedding clothing, and she'd hired her current landlord, who was a professional tailor with a shop in Eron, to help.

She cleared her throat softly so as not to startle Jeanie. "Hey, Grams."

Jeanie took her eyes off the machine and lifted her head. "Hey, Sunshine." Her smile was vibrant, as it always was whenever she spoke to Chloe.

"You guys must have left early, judging by the fact that you're already changed and working hard."

"George wanted to get back home. He was getting uncomfortable." She rested her hand on the edge of the sewing machine. "You're home early. Thought you and Noah would stay out late."

She shrugged, "Late doing what? We already danced and ate." Her gaze shifted to the tall dressers against the wall that were filled with all kinds of fabric. "I should probably shower and help you sew. There's lots of work to do."

"You need a break. I think you deserve it after finalizing three fashion lines in less than four days."

Chloe had pulled out some designs she had drawn over the last five years and tucked away to use someday. She'd had to tweak them a bit to match current fashion trends, and hoped they would be well received by fashion houses and critics soon.

"You're probably right." She ran a hand over her face as an idea came to mind. Should she go visit Zach tonight? Her heart felt heavy at the thought. She really needed God's wisdom in this matter. She let out a slow sigh, "I think I'll take a long shower."

"And?" Jeanie always knew when Chloe was plotting something.

Chloe shrugged a shoulder. "Zach wanted to see some of my designs," she said. "I was thinking of dropping by his place tonight."

The designs were an excuse, and no doubt Jeanie knew that. "It's high time someone else besides me gets to see your designs." She gave Chloe a coy smile. "I'm sure Zach will agree with me that your designs are spectacular."

The designs could really wait – she didn't have to go there tonight.

Her indecision must have shown on her face, because Jeanie asked, "Is everything okay?"

Not really, since she was experiencing a crazy kind of attraction to a man she just met less than ten days ago. "Yes, everything is okay."

She said goodbye to her grandma and left for her bedroom down the hall. She sank onto her bed and dropped her purse to the carpeted floor before she buried her face in her hands.

Tonight had been her fifth date with Noah, and instead of drawing closer to the man, she was slightly drifting away from him. She needed to tell Noah how she felt.

While Chloe showered, thoughts of Zach continued to torture her mind. What had happened to him, and why had he left the dance early without saying goodbye? She pulled on her dark leggings and slid into a white top, then added a loose teal cardigan, long enough to hang past her knees.

She texted Zach.

Why did you leave in the middle of the dance?

She waited for a response, eyes glued to the screen. After what seemed like two long minutes and no response, she reached for her ankle boots from her dresser.

Maybe she would pick up a cheesecake for him, too, since he'd not eaten dessert when he came to her house for dinner. She rolled her eyes at herself. That was the cheesiest excuse she'd ever used to see a guy.

Thirty minutes later, Chloe inhaled the fresh air of the quiet countryside, and allowed the familiar sounds of beauty in the vast land to soothe her as she drove the familiar road to Zach's grandparents' house.

Once parked in the driveway of a detached garage, which was 200 feet from the main house, Chloe took a moment to breathe in the crisp air as she gazed around the meadow. In the spring, the meadow always sprouted with colorful flowers, and memories of her childhood sprouted–the long summer days spent here.

To the far side of the property was another building, which had once been a cabin used as the main house. Then, after the newer house was built, siding had been added to the cabin as it was renovated to serve as the community church. Now that the church occupied a larger building in another location, the former cabin stood vacant.

Cheesecake in hand, Chloe took the first step toward the house and her heart jolted. *Lord, I should have prayed before showing up here. Am I doing the right thing?*

She really had no idea what she was doing, except that she took another slow step, her confidence thinning with each step, until she was standing in front of the two story stone house with an expansive porch. Having lived here for several years, she knew the back had a wide deck and a spectacular mountain view.

She raised her hand to knock, but paused before striking the door.

When the door opened, a beautiful woman emerged and Chloe froze, being caught off guard. A brunette stood the same medium height as Chloe, with clear blue eyes and fashionably dressed. She was probably one of Zach's model friends he'd talked about.

No wonder Zach had left in the middle of the dance! This must have been the call he'd gotten.

Her chest tightened and her mind went blank.

The woman arched a brow. "Uh... hi?"

Chloe held the cake tray out to her. "I brought Zach a cheesecake. When he visited my family the other day, he didn't get the chance to eat dessert."

Didn't have the chance to eat dessert? Really?

"Hmm." The woman stared at the cake. "His favorite. I will definitely gobble some of this until he takes me out to dinner." The woman seemed more interested in the cake than the messenger herself.

If Zach didn't have a girlfriend, who was this woman?

She needed to get out of here before she looked more awkward than she already felt. "Okay, I... Bye."

"Cheesecake? Zach says they make the best food in this town," the woman said, her eyes never leaving the cake.

Chloe turned, determined not to spin her neck for a second glance.

"Oh, bye," the woman's voice came out as an afterthought.

Chloe was halfway to her car when a deep voice echoed. "Chloe, wait!"

She turned at the familiar voice. Zach was jogging toward her, dressed in basketball shorts, no shirt, a towel draped over his shoulder. Was he crazy?

She froze for a second while she gawked at his lean muscles. Her heart thundered, sending a warmth through her, and she took a slow breath before she turned her back to him. His strong arm settled on her shoulder when he caught up to her—a touch that triggered an electric jolt all the way through her body.

His green eyes explored her face and he breathed, his voice low, "Hey, you can't leave."

She studied him, drowning in eyes that were deep emerald like her favorite stone. She turned her gaze to his damp brown hair, then his face, the strong chin made more handsome by the short stubble. Afraid to stare at his bare chest, she inhaled the fresh scent of his shampoo.

"I... are you just coming out of the shower?" In case he wasn't aware of his attire, she reminded him, "You don't have a shirt on."

Unsure where to direct her gaze with him standing a whisper apart, she dropped her eyes to the misty ground and rubbed her hands on her arms against the cold air that seeped through her sweater to her skin. She should've stayed home and sewed clothes with Jeanie.

"Yes. I was getting out of the shower when I heard your voice. Hearing you say goodbye got me sprinting down those stairs instantly. If I started looking for a shirt, you'd be gone by now. I couldn't take the chance of not seeing you today."

What did he mean by that?

He rubbed the towel over his damp hair, then wrapped it around his shoulders to cover his upper body. "Is that better?"

"Yes. Thank you."

"You and I know that you can only eat one slice of cheesecake because of the extra calories. I can't eat all that cake by myself."

She shrugged. "You have company. I'm sure the two of you can manage a cheesecake, or have leftovers." She turned. "I really better get going."

He clasped her hand to pull her towards him. "Not happening," he said. "You have to meet my sister."

Sister? What a relief! The tension in her chest melted. She still wasn't sure she would connect with the model, based on their brief awkward interaction. "I don't think she wants to meet me anyway, maybe another time."

"There will not be another time," he said. "Plus, if I could sit through Cynthia's glare during an entire dinner, you can definitely handle my sister for a few minutes."

She stared at him for a moment, considering his invitation.

His breathing hadn't eased. She noticed the pulse in his throat. Was it from his jogging to catch up with her, or was he feeling the same way she did?

His brows shot up, questioning, waiting for her response. She threw her head back and groaned, her voice weak when she spoke. "Have I told you how much I don't like you?"

"Hmm, not really." He smiled, a genuine smile just for her. Perhaps emboldened by her softened features, he tightened his grip on her and started to walk back. "If I told you that you looked beautiful in your purple dress tonight, would you hold that against me?"

The compliment sent warmth right through her. "Maybe."

"What if I told you that you're breathtaking, and that you remind me of a princess in my field of dreams?"

He sure knew all the right words to say to a girl. Her body aflame, she squeaked, "That's a fairy tale, Zach."

"I'm glad that you're not a fairy tale, Chloe. For that reason, I think we could work out some way to get you to like me."

"You're incorrigible." She rolled her eyes.

He chuckled, "Incorrigible?"

Chloe didn't breathe normally until Zach dropped her hand when they arrived at the front door.

CHAPTER 7

The afternoon sunlight streamed through the window of Leticia's living room, illuminating Chloe's soft profile as she slid the measuring tape down the length of Zach's arm.

Her hands brushed the inside of his wrist, shocking every nerve in his body. Standing so close to her, the soft, flowery scent of her conditioner or perfume filled his senses. Zach swallowed, his mouth suddenly dry when she pressed the tape firmly on both ends to make sure it was a good fit.

"Thirty-seven," she dictated to Leticia, who sat on the floral brown sofa crouched over the coffee table, writing down the measurements.

Zach had done the same when Chloe took Leticia's measurements for a dress Chloe was making for the woman to wear to Sofia's wedding.

Not meeting Zach's gaze, Chloe said softly, "I need to measure your shoulders."

Chloe stood on tippy toes and touched him as she ran the measuring tape from one shoulder to the other, measuring the width over the polo-shirt he'd worn for church this morning.

Breathe, he had to remind himself. He wished Leticia could break the silence, but the old woman stayed hunched over the coffee table, busy making endless lists in between jotting down the measurements.

Chloe uttered the number to Leticia without lifting her head to meet the woman's gaze. Or was she avoiding Zach's scrutiny?

The moment of his undoing was when she laced the measuring tape around his neck, leaving a trail of heat in its wake. He found himself staring at her, maybe staring at her lips, and perhaps she felt him looking, if her trembling fingers at the base of his collar-bone were any indication.

"Stop looking at me like that," she whispered to Zach, then spoke up to Leticia. "Sixteen."

Leticia suddenly lifted her head. "What number should I write again?"

Chloe dropped a hand to her forehead and winced. "I think it was fourteen, or was it fifteen?"

Zach wasn't any help, since he hadn't been paying attention to measurements either. "I think fourteen, maybe?"

"Perhaps it's best you do that again," Leticia suggested.

This was the reason Zach was glad that Chloe had suggested taking measurements at Leticia's house instead of his place. This crazy attraction between them didn't seem to respect any boundaries whatsoever.

Leticia had invited them to lunch after church, and Chloe had taken advantage of the time to take both Zach and Leticia's measurements. After lunch, Leticia's husband had been called to another emergency to rescue a cow that was choking.

After the measurements were all taken, they settled into the living room. Zach sat in a recliner and Chloe flopped on the sofa across from him. Leticia brought them chocolate pie and returned to the kitchen.

Zach balanced the small plate in his palm. "Tell me more about my property. I can't ignore the feeling that it holds some meaning to you."

When Chloe had stopped by on Valentine's Day, she had showed Zach and Addie where the water heater was in case they needed to adjust the water temperature. She also knew the ins and outs of the house, and Zach hadn't missed how fondly she'd spoken about the cabinets that had been installed twenty years ago. The way she'd run a hand over the bookshelf and certain pieces of furniture had made Addie and Zach exchange glances.

"I grew up there." Her response pulled Zach out of his thoughts. "Or at least most of my childhood memories reside in that place." She glanced down at her plate and passed the fork over the pie.

Zach forked the soft pie and lifted a delicious bite to his mouth, giving her time to continue her revelation.

"I was almost four when our house caught on fire. We lost everything — except not everything, since we were alive." She stared at the purple wall paper. "Your grandparents took us in and we lived at The Meadow, at least that's what I call your grandparents' house. We stayed there for ten years, until the new house was rebuilt."

She told him how her grandma had worked hard at selling quilts, supplying them to tourist shops all over Colorado so they could afford to get their house rebuilt. She let out a sigh and stared at him before asking something completely unrelated.

"Any offers on your house yet?" Her expression was unreadable.

Zach cleared his throat. "Sofia thinks that it will sell faster if everything's out of the house, and also if I can get a couple of walls fixed in there."

He'd left Noah a message to call him back, but he hadn't heard back from him yet. Zach ran a hand over his face. "Things are moving much slower than I'd like, but I'm glad it's given me the opportunity to get to know some people." Her in particular.

Although he wanted an excuse to spend time with her, his next words came from a sincere desire to benefit her, too. "I've been dreading going through all the boxes at the house."

Her brown eyes flew back to his, searching, and he cleared his throat before continuing. "Was wondering if you would like to come by and go through some of those things with me, since you have some memories there, too."

She turned her gaze back to the wall and Zach wondered if his suggestion had been a terrible idea. "I don't mean to impose, but I thought it would…"

"I'd love that," she said softly. "Thank you!"

She finally reached for her plate from the coffee table and set it on her lap. "Mondays are always slow. I don't know if tomorrow is too soon for you."

He didn't expect to do it that soon, but hey, why not? "Tomorrow sounds great!"

He tilted the glass of water to his lips, then set it back on the table. "So two things you didn't tell me right off - that you cleaned my house, and that you grew up at the same house. How come you didn't say anything the first day we met?"

"You didn't ask."

He chuckled. "Like I would know. I'm the newcomer, remember?"

"At this point, I wouldn't consider you a newcomer, really. You're just soaking up this newcomer thing, aren't you?"

He shrugged. "A guy can only get so much attention."

Their forks clinked on their plates just as Leticia returned with a pitcher of ice water. Zach held his glass out for a refill.

Chloe stared at her half eaten pie. "Thank you, Leticia. You make such delicious everything."

The old woman chuckled. "Oh, my dear girl, you're always very encouraging."

Zach cleared his throat and stared at his empty plate. "Chloe's right, you're a great cook."

"I hope Garth will return in time to enjoy his pie," Leticia said. "I'm happy he'll get a break next week when Doctor Cami fills in."

"Is he still going horseback riding?" Zach leaned back in the chair.

"Great memory." Leticia smiled. "I'd forgotten he mentioned that when you were here the other day."

As they chatted, Leticia talked about her son, Pete Haldem. He was a war veteran, and was struggling with PTSD. Her gaze met Chloe's. "That was brave of you to break in the fight. You could've been hurt."

It all registered with Zach–the fight, and the thrill of excitement that went through him as he watched the bold beauty silence two furious men. His eyes found Chloe's, and he breathed, "I watched the entire scene with my own eyes."

Chloe scrunched up her face.

"Thanks for saving him from going back to jail," Leticia said.

Dismissing the compliment, Chloe responded, "You know Pete does whatever he wants, jail or no jail. I couldn't say anything to stop him if he wanted to…"

"You seem to be the only person to get through to him."

Did Leticia's tone hint at matchmaking for Pete and Chloe? Zach tried to ignore the slight pang of jealousy creeping into his heart.

He and Chloe listened to the old woman prattle on about how distant their relationship with their son had been for the last two years. She then talked about her deceased cats, particularly the recently deceased cat, Tigger, that she'd rescued from a bad situation. A tender smile formed on her lips. "She was quite a handful!"

She shared several fond memories, and Chloe listened intently, hands on her lap. "She loved to kick her litter out of her litter box once she did her kitty business."

Chloe's eyes expressed genuine concern when Leticia spoke of how much she missed having Tigger under her feet all the time. Zach had nothing against cats, but he preferred live ones to listening to stories about felines that had gone back to their Maker. All the more reason for him to be impressed by Chloe's kindness in indulging the old lady's reminiscing.

Zach leaned back and smiled when Chloe burst into laughter as Leticia described the games Tigger had played, and how she liked bringing Leticia dead mice and other small animals as a way to show her love. Chloe asked several questions about Tigger that led to the woman pulling out video recordings of her cats.

"You will have to sit on the sofa to be able to see the TV." Leticia steered Zach to the sofa, where he sank next to Chloe. When their shoulders brushed and she didn't move or flinch, he felt a radiating warmth inside, a feeling of home and comfort—a familiar feeling always present in Chloe's presence. There was no place he'd rather be than sitting beside her, even if it was watching memories of deceased cats on TV.

The morning rays shone through the glass windows of Chloe's boutique as she glared at the Excel spreadsheet on her laptop. She still needed to keep track of where her samples were, and what companies on her list she needed to send samples too.

Sitting two inches from her on the sofa was her associate Jules, phone in hand. They'd already gone through their morning routine of looking at their inventory, the kind of materials needed for the designs, and had also discussed what else needed to be done before the fashion show.

"Wait." Jules, still holding her phone, lifted her hand up and her eyes widened. "The photographer said that there's been a cancellation for the entire Memorial Day weekend, and we're in."

Chloe took her eyes off the computer screen and met Jules' half smile, which rarely made an appearance. Ever since Jules' return to Eron, it seemed as if she had an inner battle going on——a burden she carried alone, unwilling to unleash it on anyone.

"That's such a relief!" Chloe put her hand to her chest. One of the best photographers in Colorado, who normally did fashion shows, was booked a year in advance. When they'd first approached him about the fashion show, he was already booked for the entire weekend.

Jules had been working hard to make calls to several vendors and volunteers they would need for the show.

"Have I told you how grateful I am to have you as my business partner?" Chloe smiled at Jules, knowing it drove her crazy whenever anybody praised her. "Thank you for your hard work."

Jules rolled her eyes and turned back to her phone. "What do you expect me to do when you're paying me?"

Jules' organizational skills and her cool head when working under pressure came in handy on such occasions. She and Chloe had been best friends while growing up, until Jules had fled with her mom to another town. It wasn't until three months ago that Jules had returned, and Chloe asked her to partner with her at the boutique.

"I haven't looked on Facebook lately." Chloe stole a glimpse at the clock on the computer, since she'd been counting down the hours until she would see Zach, ever since they'd departed yesterday. "How are we doing?"

"Speaking of which, I think that Hottie's sister is doing a great job with getting the word out." Jules' nickname for Zach was Hottie. She scrolled through her phone and leaned closer to Chloe to share the new growth of their Facebook page.

When Chloe had visited with Zach's sister a few days ago, she had been thrilled to learn that Chloe was a fashion designer. Zach had been right about Addie being in love with designer clothing and she had spent the first thirty minutes or so after meeting Chloe just talking about current trends and wanting to know which styles Chloe designed. She said she would be Chloe's advocate in Hollywood and LA.

Addie had turned out to be more chatty than Chloe had expected. That night, they visited and laughed together, and Chloe ended up joining her and Zach for a late dinner. Addie was hungry and craved American food, which had been Zach's request, too. Chloe only ordered pie when she took them to Eron's local diner, which Zach and his sister loved so much that Zach planned to go back.

Chloe returned her attention to their Facebook page and shook her head, not believing that they'd moved from 200 likes to 6,000 in just one week. So far, they were still behind with RSVPs for the event, but she was hopeful that some of the Facebook fans would turn into attendees to the show.

Not sure whether to be excited or to panic, she let out a slow breath. "Now we just need to figure out space. In case we have over one hundred outsiders show up in Eron for the fashion show."

"We can set up a tent in the parking lot for the overflow from the boutique," Jules suggested, perhaps forgetting that Colorado got late spring snow storms at times. "Just so we don't spend money we don't have."

Chloe's brows furrowed, unsure of the venue and how parking would affect it. "What if we get over two hundred people?"

"Let's take one day at a time. We'll worry about that when we get to it." Jules rose and shoved her phone into her jeans pocket. "I need to go and get some real coffee before you leave for Hottie's place. God knows how much trouble you're in already by falling for a guy who's leaving."

Chloe met Jules' knowing look. Though abrasive, Jules was straight forward, and Chloe liked that. She was also Chloe's best friend, she and Sofia. Although Chloe had tried to deny her feelings for Zach, Jules had ignored her protestations. "I think I'm falling for him, and I have a feeling that he likes me, too. It's complicated because everyone assumes that I'm with Noah, yet I'm not, really." She slumped her shoulders. "What am I going to do?"

Jules rolled her eyes. "Boo hoo, poor Chloe! I'm sure you're loving all this attention from two handsome men competing for you." Her dye-streaked bun bounced when she scratched the center of her hair. "Just tell Sweet Pea that he's not your type. Whether Hottie is leaving or not, I think you and Sweet Pea are far from making that 'couple.'" She made air quotes with her fingers.

Chloe arched her brows. "Since when did you start calling Noah Sweet Pea?"

"The moment I met him," she admitted. "I better get going."

"You're sure you will manage today without me?"

Jules parked her hand on her hip. "Unless the new followers on Facebook all decide to show up before the fashion show, then I won't need your sweet smile for the customers." Dropping her hand, she said, "Just in case they show up, I had already thought it through and didn't feel like scaring customers. That's why I recruited Hank, so he can put on his smiling face to reel in the customers while I handle cash transactions."

"Will he not be working at the hotel?"

Jules shrugged. "He said they're flexible with him."

Hank was outgoing enough, with a good sales pitch. "That's nice of him to help."

While Chloe responded to her emails, the door chime caused her to lift her eyes and meet Sofia's big brother's frown as he walked into the shop, his sandy blonde hair slicked to the side, dressed in a perfectly fitted suit as always.

"Hi, Brent."

"Hey, Chloe." He set a bag of something aromatic on the coffee table in front of Chloe.

"I just wish Sofie would stop sending me to that sorry excuse for a deli." He brushed his hands together as if erasing the dirt from the bag he'd just set on the table, his face wrinkled in disgust. "They can't even afford to buy normal napkins."

The attention Chloe gave Brent was divided as she read another email from one of her fabric vendors. She tore her eyes off the computer to respond to his complaint. "I'm sorry your experience wasn't as great…"

"Sofie is threatening to stop helping with my projects if I don't model. It's not good for my image or the company. I'm a CEO, for crying out loud, not a model!"

Brent Wise and his family, with the exception of Sofia, dreaded socializing with people who were not in their wealthy social status. Modeling would not only force him to mingle with the town locals, but it would demean him, since he was the CEO of Wise Enterprise. Even if she needed a model, Chloe didn't want to pressure anybody into it.

"You don't have to stress about it, Brent. I will tell Sofia to not pressure you." His presence could help draw in the wealthy crowds from his circle, though. "Maybe you can invite some of your clients and friends."

He seemed to think about it for a moment, before he slowly nodded. "I think I can do that." He then tugged at his tie and pointed to the bag. "Can you just let Sofie know that I got her pastries over there?"

Chloe nudged her chin towards the stairs. "Why don't you take it to her so you can say hi."

He hesitated before he turned to the stairs, almost bumping into someone who was coming down.

"Oh, it's you," Brent mumbled to Keisha, Sofia's future sister-in-law.

Chloe half listened to the exchange as she typed a response to an email.

"I thought…" Keisha stammered. Chloe couldn't blame her for being nervous, since Brent and Sofia's fiancé Trevor didn't get along. "I...thought we could be friends, since your sister is getting married to..."

"Your brother?"

Chloe had to take her eyes off the computer to peer at Brent's glare.

"Do I look like I'm looking for a friend, Keisha? Huh?"

Keisha let out an exasperated sigh and spoke without meeting Brent's eyes. "You don't have to be a jerk." She stomped all the way through the shop and out of the door.

Chloe closed the opened windows on the laptop, and shook her head in amusement at how the twenty-something had stood up for herself against Brent.

Remembering that she had more important things to do than listen to arguments, Chloe pressed the power button to shut down her laptop. She needed to buy some photo albums from the country store, and then go back home to pick up the chicken Jeanie was making for Zach.

Jeanie had felt bad for Zach that night when he'd joined them for dinner and had a tummy ache. He then had to put up with Cynthia's rudeness, which at times came with her being irritable due to not being able to do things she wanted to anymore.

When the door dinged, announcing Jules' return with a styrofoam cup in her hand, Chloe smiled in anticipation of what the day held. Butterflies suddenly fluttered in her belly as her mind wandered to the green eyed man she was going to spend the rest of the day with.

She hoped as they shuffled through boxes that held memories of their pasts, they could be set free for a future of unimaginable possibilities.

.

CHAPTER 8

Tote bag in hand, Chloe slammed her car door with a thud and blinked into the bright blue sky of early March. Not only was she thankful for Eron's mild winter this year, she was grateful for today, with its promise of a chance to go back in time.

To the west side of a vast meadow was a large cabin, which was on the same forty acre property she knew so well. A place she considered home, she was torn that it would be sold to someone else very soon. Her heart tightened at the thought of the home falling into the hands of a developer.

She turned to the east, an open meadow lined with aspens in the distance. In three months or less, the golden meadow would be a vibrant green, erupting with pink and purple wildflowers. She smiled as she remembered the long summer days when she would run through the field of flowers as a child, chasing butterflies and picking flowers to make headbands for her hair.

She took a deep breath and started walking towards the generous porch of the two-story stone house.

The door swung open while she was still a distance away and Zach appeared in the doorway, dressed in loose shorts and a v-neck, short sleeved white t-shirt. With a guitar slung across his chest, he grinned at her before his eyes shifted back to the guitar and he set a thumb to the strings.

His hand struck the first chord, and the next, strumming more chords before he started singing.

Chloe lost her balance, almost tripping at the sound of his deep, rich voice when he started singing a song she recognized. *Here comes the Sun,* by the Beatles. His smile widening, he continued serenading her, swinging his head from side to side in time to the music as he picked the guitar strings.

She slowed her steps as she neared the stairs to the front porch, keeping her gaze on the musician. Her jaw dropped in awe as Zach continued strumming the strings gently with his fingertips, his lean frame and guitar blocking the entrance.

She smiled and stared at him while he moved his head in rhythm with the song. Chloe's heart warmed and lifted all at the same time.

When the song ended, he let the final chord linger, then bent to lean the guitar against the door jamb. Lifting his head, he smiled at her, a smile genuinely meant for her, and it made her body tremble.

He placed a hand to his chest. "Welcome, Princess!" He gave a dramatic bow before he stepped forward to take the tote from her hand.

To Chloe, a princess was someone who had servants to tend to them, and things handed to them whenever they wanted. "Why do you call me princess? I'm far from that."

"You're the most princessy person I've ever met." He waved her into the house ahead of him.

Chloe took in a shuddering sigh, overwhelmed by his easy going manner, the genuine way he complimented her, as if it were an everyday kind of thing to say.

She said instead, "the song was...you have a very nice voice." *Did she just say that out loud?* She ran a hand over her warm face, racking her mind to come up with anything less embarrassing. "Are you always this endearing?"

So much for less embarrassment. She wished she could snatch the words back when she remembered his response the last time she had called him endearing.

He picked up the guitar and kicked the door closed behind them. "Glad you still find me endearing."

"Don't pump yourself up, Doctor."

"I will take that as a compliment." He set the guitar and bag on the kitchen counter. "What do you have in this bag? It smells amazing."

She moved beside him and they both reached into the bag at the same time. Their hands brushed and Chloe's pulse shot up.

She instinctively snatched her hand out of the bag. She then moved to stand by the window and leaned against the counter.

"My grandma made you some chicken." Her voice faltered and she tried to make it as normal as possible. "Coming to visit a new-in-town bachelor, she was worried that you would not feed me."

"She's a wise woman." He opened the container and took a peek inside, sniffing appreciatively.

"So, you took music while studying to become a doctor?" Chloe asked as Zach set the chicken in the refrigerator.

He shrugged and closed the refrigerator. "That's one of the perks of being raised by an actress. I took music lessons and played all sorts of instruments from a very young age." He trailed off for a moment, and his gaze became distant. "I got to skip fourth and sixth grades. It was always hard for me to make friends who weren't my own age." Then he turned to her with an ironic grin. "Except the acting friends came pretty easy, since none of them cared about my nerdy personality. Sounds pathetic, right?"

"I think that's... amazing." He was intelligent and talented and sensitive, and so much more.

"Thanks."

She asked about his doctor friends he traveled with, and he mostly talked about Rahul, who was currently visiting his family in India.

"He's one of the best ophthalmologists I know, and he has a heart of gold. I watched him treat several people who'd been blind for years, yet all they needed was a simple cataract surgery to restore their sight."

"How did you meet your friend Rahul?"

He scratched his stubbled chin and stared at the off-white wall. "I met him at the first hospital where I did my residency. We were working together on a patient with my attending doctor at the time, who was getting ready to go to Indonesia and he told us about the scarcity of doctors in several places."

He leaned against the refrigerator and crossed one leg over the other. "That doctor asked us,'Do you ever wonder why God has made you the way you are, and how are you going to use the gifts that he has given you?' That's when I realized that there was more to life than living for myself, and there was more to my career than just making money. That made an impact on Rahul, too, and we've been working together ever since."

The sun streamed through the window, sending warmth through the house. Chloe turned to stare out the window, digesting what Zach had just shared. A couple of deer were grazing in the meadow.

"Come see this." She motioned to him, and he came to stand beside her.

"Wow!' he said, his breath warm against her hair. "What a view!"

"I assume these are the first deer you've seen since you got here?" She turned away from the window and stepped back, creating a gap between them.

"I wasn't looking through the window that much. I've been kind of busy with all the invitations to people's homes lately." He gave her a mischievous smile.

Although several seniors had invited him to their homes when he'd played bingo with them, Chloe knew that he hadn't been at anyone's homes except Chloe's and his neighbor Leticia's.

"We better get to work." She walked to the living room. "Where would you like to start?"

"Shouldn't we eat lunch first?"

"It's only ten."

He groaned and threw his head back. "Okay, but if I pass out, I'm blaming you." He ran a hand through his wavy brown hair and sauntered to the stairs. "Let's start with the mystery boxes, and then we'll tackle the pictures next."

"I brought some albums to organize the pictures. I can get them out of the car when we're ready for them."

"Only if I pay for those albums."

She'd not paid a lot for the albums, but she didn't plan to argue with him, since she'd put on a huge argument when he'd insisted on paying her for cleaning his house, and for the few items she'd bought to put in the house. "We'll see."

Zach crouched, dodging a cobweb, as he trekked downstairs with Chloe following. He flipped on the switch, and bright lights illuminated the room.

She stilled when her eyes landed on one of the two bedrooms downstairs, one next to the bathroom. She and Jeanie had stayed downstairs when they'd moved in with the Erons. Everything seemed so familiar; the smell and the vivid memories of Christmas stories and laughter echoed in the back of her mind.

"Everything okay?" Zach pulled a black trash bag from the box.

"Yeah." her voice barely audible, and she pointed her chin to the room stacked with boxes against the wall. "Can you believe this used to be my bedroom?"

He stepped beside her. "It looks different with all the boxes, doesn't it?"

She gave a silent nod.

"Let's start in this room then." His hands patted against the wall searching for the switch.

"I know where it is." She reached past him and flicked on the light in the small bedroom.

A spider crept along one of the boxes. When she'd cleaned the house, she had swept all the floors, but she hadn't had the time to dust the two bedrooms.

Zach spread the black trash bag on the hardwood floor, then added another beside it, and another, until he'd created an adequate work space. "In case we get tired and need to sit," he explained. "I'm used to sitting on the floors in people's homes when I travel, since many people in those countries don't have furniture at all."

Chloe couldn't imagine a house without a single piece of furniture in it. "Not even a chair?"

"Nothing."

She was about to ask another question when he reached for the top box from the high stack. As he stretched his arms upward, a gap opened between his t-shirt and the waistband of his low-slung shorts, giving Chloe a brief flash of his tanned skin. Her mouth went dry, which was okay because she'd forgotten what she was going to say anyway.

When he set the box on the floor, Chloe crouched to open it, then had to bury her face in her elbow when the dust from the box brought on a fit of sneezing.

"Bless you!"

"Thank you." She tugged open the flaps and pulled out several pieces of clothing. Zach tackled a separate box, which also held mostly clothes, which they put into a few of the black bags to donate to Salvation Army.

They moved through more boxes, each tackling one at a time, setting aside anything of interest, until only one small box was left–Zach's.

"Look at this?" He held up a crochet doll with black yarn for hair curls.

Chloe's mouth opened, and she smiled as she took it from his hand. "I remember this doll." She tenderly brushed it free of dust, then put the doll to her chest and plopped onto the floor. "This was my first doll. Grams told me I got it when I was four years old. Guess I used to carry it everywhere with me."

When she shifted her gaze to Zach, warm green eyes peered down at her. He then brought the entire box and set it in front of her. "Looks like all these go together."

He sank onto the floor next to her, stretching his long legs out and crossing them at the ankles.

As Chloe rummaged through the rest of the box, she discovered several mementos from her childhood she'd not seen for a long time. School reports, her kindergarten graduation certificate, and various sports medals Jeanie had tucked away, and perhaps had forgotten their whereabouts.

She then reached for a picture album with a straw looking cover and brushed off the dust. She opened the frail pages and saw photos of a dark skinned little girl, four or five years old, hands on hips, flower garland around her head. Chloe remembered making the flower crowns from the flowers in the meadow as a child. Her eyes flew to the cursive notes written in blue ink on the bottom paper section of the picture. It read *Chloe Love, 4 years old.*

Zach leaned closer. "What a cutie! I can tell she was a handful, too."

Chloe nudged him with her elbow and he gave a low chuckle, which should've cleared the tension, but it made her belly quiver instead.

She focused on the album as she turned to the next page, which held a photo of her and Jeanie, then found more pictures of Jeanie and her friends on the next page. When she flipped to another page, one image caused Zach and Chloe to stare at each other before returning their eyes to the album.

It was a group picture with Zach's grandparents and Jeanie. A little boy around six or seven stood right in front of them, grinning mischievously. Zach gasped. "Is that me?"

Chloe nodded slowly. "Grandma had said that there were a few pictures of you somewhere in this house."

"She said I came here when I was six, and then when I was seven, too?" His voice rose wistfully as he traced the outline of himself in the picture.

"That's right." Chloe flipped open the next page, revealing a picture that drew their attention until their heads almost touched as they studied it. She could feel his warm breath, and his fresh scent intoxicated her.

Chloe and Zach, the notes read. The picture showed a little Caucasian boy in a meadow, handing the crochet doll to a crying Black girl.

Zach pointed to Chloe's doll in the picture. "There's your doll." His voice was more raspy.

Chloe's hand flew to her lips. Although her grandma had told her that Zach had played with her a couple of summers in their childhood, the conversation had not registered until now.

She turned to Zach, who seemed frozen in place. "My grandma also told me that you and I shared this room when you came to visit."

Zach's eyes widened. "I can't believe it."

They both seemed to suddenly realize how close they were leaning towards each other, and Zach quickly scooted back to lean against the wall. Chloe did the same, keeping about two inches between them.

"Do you want to hear something strange?' Zach's face was serious when he spoke.

Chloe bobbed a fast nod. "Yes."

"The moment I stepped into this house and walked down the stairs, everything seemed so familiar. It felt as if I'd been here before."

"Like déjà vu?"

"Exactly!" His face wrinkled. "Do you want to hear something even more crazy?"

"What's that?"

His voice was low when he spoke. "From the first time I saw you in December, I felt as if I knew you. Even the last two months while I was in the Philippines, my heart kept pulling me back to you, as if you held something I needed to know." His soft eyes found hers, and his voice fell to a whisper. "It's like I found a part of me in somebody else. Like I found my new best friend, and something more at the same time – someone I can confide in...Thank you for coming...for going through this stuff with me."

Chloe swallowed, suddenly hot, her mind blank. She didn't know what to say, except that she felt drawn to him for no apparent reason. She was grateful for the chance to browse through her past with him, and oddly wanted him to be a part of her life, her future.

How that could happen with a man set to leave town, she had no idea.

If Zach wasn't falling head over heels for Chloe Love, then he needed a psychiatric consultation to figure out why he felt so connected to her in a way he'd never thought possible.

He pushed the top button of his flannel shirt through its hole and stared at the vast space in front of his house. He and Chloe had spent the last six hours going through boxes of things, before they took a break to gobble the fried chicken. They had then looked through more pictures of his family as they slid them into the photo albums.

He'd completely lost track of time, until she reminded him it was four o'clock and they needed to get to his grandparents' grave site, something Chloe had suggested last night when she texted him. The six hours of work had only felt like five minutes, and it had made the work more enjoyable.

If only he wasn't leaving–worse yet, if only he wasn't second guessing about selling the house. After hearing Chloe's fond memories of this place, Zach needed to pray for wisdom and clarity, just in case selling the house wasn't what God wanted him to do.

He hadn't told Chloe that he'd received a text from Sofia, last night. Someone wanted to buy twenty five acres of the land, but not the house. He wasn't interested in that kind of buyer, anyway, since he would rather sell the entire forty acres and the house with it, if it came down to it, and mostly sell it to someone who would appreciate the house.

"Zach." Chloe's voice pulled him out of his thoughts. He met her hotter- than- fire smile when she handed him a bouquet of pink roses she'd brought to take to the grave site. "Will you please hold these while I zip up my sweater?"

He stared down at her maroon leggings and the unzipped teal sweatshirt. Compelled to touch her, his feet led him closer to her, and he placed his hands down to her zipper. He could see her eyes widen in fascination, when he pulled the zipper up.

He placed both hands on her shoulders, and her heart thumped heavily when his gaze dropped down to her lips. A tension filled moment hung between them, and Zach blinked. Dropping his hands, he said, "All set," then took the flowers from her.

"I take it that pink roses are your favorite?" He arched a brow. "You don't strike me as a rose kind of girl."

She started walking to the east side of the meadow, and Zach moved in step to her side.

"I like all kinds of flowers," she said. "However, pink roses were your grandma's favorites. She told me that, on their first date, your grandpa went to buy her red roses, but the store had run out of red roses, so he bought the pink instead, and after that, he started buying her pink roses on the anniversary of their first date."

How interesting! Zach thought.

"Since you seem to know a thing or two about flowers, what kind of flowers do you think I like?"

"I can tell you're a tulip or ranunculus kind of person."

She spun around and stopped walking, her lips parted. "How did you know that ranunculus are my favorites?"

He chuckled, pleased that he had guessed her favorite flower. He really didn't know much about plants, except what he'd picked up from his mom's gardener. The Chinese man knew a lot about flowers and plants, and each time Zach spoke to him, all the man talked about was plants and their meaning.

Zach said, "The ranunculus flower is a symbol of radiant charm and attractiveness, regardless of its color." She was both those things and more.

"You're the charming one, I'd say." She tilted her head to meet his eyes, and as if realizing what she just said, she switched the conversation back to plants. "What about tulips?"

"True love." He went on to tell her the meanings of the few flowers that he knew.

She shook her head in amazement before turning her gaze back to the wide garden path.

Chloe's smile reached her eyes as she led the way and chattered about the flowers that grew in the meadow, Zach watching her every move. She pointed to the house on the west side of the meadow. "That used to be the main house. Then they renovated it to be used as the church, until the new church was finished. They then used it to host events in the community."

"Speaking of events, where are you hosting your fashion show?"

She stopped walking and turned to him. "At the boutique."

His brows shot up. "Not sure if Addie mentioned to you, but she's rounded up several people, and word is buzzing. We may have to shuttle people into town due to traffic."

She bit her lower lip. "I don't know, Zach. I guess we might add a tent or something. I haven't figured out all the details yet."

Zach's gaze drifted back to the house on the opposite side of his property. He'd not been inside it, but since Chloe mentioned it once being an event center, an idea formed in his mind. Perhaps she could use that, but he would have to make sure it was in great condition before he offered. That would also mean that he would need to hold off on selling the place or having a closing date until after her event was over.

He surveyed the wide land. There was plenty of room for people to park their cars, more than at her boutique's location. Since the aspen trees were far away from the property, maybe a shuttle could bring people back here if it came down to it.

He'd been so caught up in his plans that he hadn't noticed that Chloe had already taken off further. When his eyes found her, her arms were spread out wide, as if she were in a special place.

As if sensing his eyes on her, she dropped her hands to her sides and turned to him smiling. "You're walking like a snail. You coming?"

"I'm just enjoying the view." She made for a special sight. He quickened his steps to catch up with her, his tennis shoes sinking into the soft earth as he breathed in the crisp air. Thankfully he'd changed into jeans, or he would be freezing.

A chipmunk scampered across the path, and several deer milled about in the distance. The sound of birds chirping broke the silence of the land; visible signs of spring slowly emerging.

Further in the distance, the mountains that surrounded the entire town were still brushed with snow.

Though neither of them could see all the homes around them, Chloe obviously knew the twists and turns of the property as she pointed out the various rocks she had played on with her childhood friends. She mentioned Zach's neighbors by name, and knew all their children.

"The McGregors live on the northwest side of you. The Movellas used to live on the other side of Leticia's, but they are now full-time missionaries in Peru."

As they strolled along, Zach inhaled the sweet fragrance of Chloe's hair, and he faltered his steps to let her take the lead—an excuse to study her slender frame. The soft breeze fluttered her silky dark hair that she wore unbound and free. Even while they'd worked, she'd kept her hair free of any hair ties, and he'd been tempted to feel its softness when the scent of her conditioner had engulfed him.

They were surrounded by leafless aspens, yet Zach's mood was anything but bleak in Chloe's presence. He felt fulfilled, exhilarated, and wished this day could go on forever.

"I don't think we will ever make it to the grave site and back in two days at the pace you're going."

She turned briefly to see him wink at her. He didn't mind staying out here for days, or years even, as long as she was with him. He didn't even want this day to come to an end, but he had to savor the fading warmth of the day, which wouldn't last for another hour.

Reaching for her cool hand, he wrapped it in one of his, holding onto the roses with his other hand.

"Can you come back again so that we can…" *Do what?* He couldn't think, not when her warm brown eyes searched his. "Maybe come back to …" He dropped her hand and ran it through his hair, then groaned at his sudden stuttering.

"I have to pack for my move soon," she said.

"When are you moving?"

"Next Wednesday. I'm taking the day off. Jules is going to run the shop for me."

"I'll help you move," he offered.

She hesitated before responding, "You don't have to. Noah is bringing his truck to help transport my items."

Just like that, Zach's elation vanished.

He hoped that Chloe didn't notice his clenched fist. He had avoided talking about Noah the entire day. Whatever she was to Noah, she seemed to stare at Zach with the same intensity with which he stared at her. If social media was right in saying that she and Noah had never shared a kiss, that's all Zach needed to stay afloat. At least, he tried not to dwell on the thought of Noah kissing Chloe, but his chest tightened at the possibility.

Who gets the first kiss with the golden girl? Zach or Noah? the post had said. Even though Zach didn't care much for gossip, he'd been frequenting the town's social media site lately, since he'd been named on the page. He also wondered at times, who was always on the look-out to know if Chloe was kissing anyone or not.

Either way, he reminded himself of the great time he'd had with her today, and he slowly uncurled his fist. "Okay, then. What time is your move?"

"Maybe nine or so, not really sure."

Not wanting to impose at the moment, Zach made a mental note of the moving day and time.

"Dad said that his MRI showed several spinal deformities, and perhaps scoliosis?" Her sudden change of subject jolted Zach from his thoughts.

He had called George to let him know that he would pass the MRI results to Dr. Garth when he returned from his horseback riding ventures.

"He will just need a spinal fusion to restore stability to his back." Which Zach had done more than ten times while abroad. "I'm sure Garth will bring in a doctor who can perform that kind of procedure."

"Thank you, for everything," she spoke before they resumed their stroll. The cemetery came into view on the other side of the wooden fence that lined the border along the east side of his property.

Zach nodded. He should be the one thanking her, and he hoped to do just that before he left town.

That night, he tossed and turned on his pillow, feeling pulled slowly by his past, the past he never knew as a child. He thought of the big house where he was sleeping, and he couldn't stop imagining it as the place where his own memories would reside.

Was that what he secretly wished for? For this house to represent his roots?

CHAPTER 9

After the early morning showers, the overcast sky held no promise of sunshine as Zach swung open the double doors. The aroma of fresh baked bread, olive oil and pungent spices that greeted him made up for the cheerless day. The Italian restaurant was becoming his favorite place to eat, not because he'd first laid eyes on Chloe here, but because he liked their food. Today's chilly temperature had put him in the mood for their tomato bisque.

Bypassing the lunch crowd ordering take out, Zach joined the end of the line of patrons waiting to be seated. He planned to eat in the restaurant before checking out the skating rink that Chloe had recommended. He might as well have some fun in town while he waited for the house to sell.

It had been almost six weeks since he'd arrived in Eron, and time was slipping away from him. He still needed two walls fixed upstairs, but the town's contractor, Noah, hadn't returned his calls.

Not that he could blame the guy–Noah considered Zach his rival, no doubt. Between the gossip on social media and Zach's random encounters with Noah at Love's Boutique whenever he came into town, the man had every reason to keep his distance from him.

Yet Noah shouldn't be afraid, because it was the other way around. Noah was the right man for Chloe. Stable, rooted in town, and Chloe's family loved and depended on him. Goodness! Even Chloe depended on him.

Zach and Chloe might have undeniable chemistry, but he doubted that would be enough for him to win her over.

The air around him suddenly crackled with energy when he shifted his gaze to one of the booths and was met by familiar brown eyes. Chloe's. What was with his quickening heart?

Frozen, he was unable to turn his gaze away from her until her date spun his head and stared at Zach. Only then was he able to shift his gaze away from Chloe.

"How many in your party?" the petite waitress asked.

"One."

She motioned for him to follow her. Chloe's gaze was focused on Noah, popping her knuckles, probably working hard to avoid glancing at Zach as he passed their table.

He was seated at a table for two, right next to Chloe and Noah's booth. A young man brought him water and took his order.

Zach's palms suddenly started sweating, not from Noah's sharp stare that he could see through the corner of his eye from time to time, but from Chloe's proximity. His neck turned against his will, and he saw Chloe still furiously popping her knuckles, a nervous habit.

Turning his focus back to his own table, Zach opened a pamphlet that had been placed on the table, which listed fascinating facts about Italy. It wasn't that he was interested in learning about Italy, but he needed a distraction to keep his eyes from wandering to Chloe.

After several minutes, his soup was brought to the table, and Zach bowed his head to pray. The silence from the next table, and the proximity, turned to awkwardness. With Noah and Chloe so silent, no doubt they were staring at him. He fought the idea of joining their booth.

He lost the battle.

Pushing his chair back, Zach pulled up and grabbed two napkins from the napkin holder. Using the napkins as potholders, he scooped his steaming hot bowl from the table and sauntered to Chloe and Noah's booth.

Chloe lowered the glass from her lips and looked up at him. Setting the glass on the table, she put a hand on her mouth and coughed into it, dribbling water onto her dress.

"Zach!" She spoke in between coughs.

"You're okay?" Zach and Noah asked at the same time.

Her hand rested on her chest and she nodded.

Satisfied that she was fine, Zach then turned to Noah. "Is it okay if I join you guys? It's a bit pathetic sitting alone in a crowded restaurant."

Noah, a muscular, dark skinned man almost the same height as Zach, gave him a quick once-over. No doubt he was going to object, but Zach was surprised by his response.

"Sure." He reluctantly pointed his hand to the space next to Chloe, who had already scooted over. They didn't have food on their table–perhaps they were still waiting for their order, or they were done eating.

Wracking his brain for a way to ease into a normal conversation, he asked, "How long have you been in this contract business, Noah?"

Noah's brows furrowed, confused at his question. "Five years?"

He was aloof at first, but knowing how people liked to talk about themselves, Zach continued to ask him questions. Noah relaxed as Zach showed genuine interest in his career, and Zach soon learned that Noah was passionate about carpentry or anything that had to do with building things. Within minutes, the trio was engaged in a casual conversation until Chloe announced she needed to get back to work.

Zach scooted out of the booth to let Chloe get past. "Thanks for lunch, Noah," she said, and Zach slid back into the booth, finally remembering his untouched soup.

"You're welcome," Noah responded to Chloe. "See you this evening?"

Zach tried to focus on his soup as he ignored the unsettled feeling in his stomach. Noah and Chloe's plans were none of his business. He forced down the bisque, keeping his eyes to the bowl and not on the beautiful woman. His face was red, no doubt, but he could only hope they would blame it on the warm soup or the temperature from the furnace in the restaurant.

"Nice to see you again, Zach."

He clanked the spoon in the porcelain bowl way too fast when he stilled. "Yeah...Was nice to see you again." His gaze swept over the mid-length, button down dress she wore over brown ankle boots—green looked good on her. He swallowed as a moment hung between them, his heart quickening. He'd almost forgotten Noah's presence until the clatter of dishes brought his attention back to his surroundings. Needing to say something, anything, to Chloe before she left, he blurted, "I've been reading 'TO KILL A MOCKINGBIRD', and I agree with you... I like the novel better than the movie."

Her eyes brightened and she pushed her dark wavy hair over her shoulder. "You did?"

He gave a slow nod. "Maybe..." He stopped his words mid sentence when he realized he was about to ask her out so they could talk about the book. He cleared his throat and said instead, "I'm going to check out that indoor skate place you recommended." *You're yapping. Will you just shut up!*

Still smiling, she said, "I'm glad you're checking out things in town."

He could sense Noah's gaze on him, so with a curt nod to Chloe, Zach said goodbye to her and picked up his spoon, only to realize the bowl was empty. When he lifted his gaze to Noah, he found the dark skinned man staring at him with a quizzical brow.

Zach needed to say something, anything, really quick. "Uh..." He cleared his throat. "You didn't return any of my calls." He rested his elbows on the table. "Maybe I have the wrong number?"

Ignoring his question entirely, Noah said, "I see that you're getting comfortable in town. I'm starting to think you've changed your mind about leaving."

By being comfortable, Noah probably meant Zach's bingo nights with the seniors, and the occasional one-on-one visits he and Chloe had made to the homes of the elderly, both of which had made it onto the social media page.

When he'd stopped by her shop yesterday while she was getting off work, Chloe was on her way to visit an old veteran, and she'd invited Zach along. They'd played scrabble but never finished the game because for each word read, the man had a war story or an old family story the words triggered.

Zach had mainly enjoyed watching Chloe listen intently to the man's stories. The girl was really good with the senior citizens. She spoke and understood their language.

"Zach!"

He blinked, snapping out of his fog. What had Noah been talking about earlier, something about him leaving? "Oh. Yes. If I can find a contractor to get the drywall done, maybe someone will be interested in buying my house and not just the property."

He shoved his bowl to the side when the server came to clear their table. "Chloe says that you're my only hope, and the best Eron has to offer."

Noah's face softened. "That's what Chloe said? That I'm the best?"

Chloe's assurance seemed to matter so much to him, as much as it mattered to Zach, too, of course. Anytime Chloe gave Zach a compliment, he felt like a kid on Christmas morning.

"Yep!" Since Chloe was uppermost in his mind, Zach's house projects didn't feel as urgent anymore. "I have this idea about Chloe's fashion show, and I was wondering if you could fix the old church on my property for her to host her fashion show in. The building could host more people than her boutique would."

Noah picked up his glass and sipped his soda, then set the glass back on the table. "Does Chloe know about this?"

"I thought I'd let her know after I see if this is the kind of work you can pull off before the show."

Noah leaned back and frowned thoughtfully for a moment before he spoke. "I will have to look at the place first. I don't think she's expecting that many people anyway."

If Chloe hadn't told Noah that she'd had more people make reservations, then Zach was not going to mention anything. "Lets just get it done regardless. It will increase the property value. You can let me know how much it will cost once you see the place."

He intended to use the money he'd saved up for rent for when he returned to LA, since he was starting to realize it would not be necessary for him to lease a place for just two months.

Zach's phone rang and he yanked it out of his jeans pocket and glanced at the screen. It was his neighbor.

"Leticia." He gave Noah an apologetic look. "Excuse me while I take this." He slid his thumb across the screen to answer the call. Before he could say 'hello,' an urgent voice spoke.

"Zach, it's Garth..." the frantic old woman's voice came in rapid breaths. "He's hurt." Her voice trailed off after she'd explained where her husband was located.

Zach was already pulling out of his seat, "I'll be right there."

He pulled a fifty dollar bill from his wallet and dropped it on the table, since that was the only bill he had on him, and he didn't want to waste time waiting for them to charge his credit card.

Noah's eyes widened. "Everything okay?"

"The town's doctor is injured."

Noah slid out of the booth. "Anything I can do?"

"Dunno! You're welcome to come with me, just in case I have to carry him to the car to get him to the hospital."

Dropping money on the table beside Zach's fifty, Noah hurried out the door after him.

Zach was grateful that Noah had come along. There was no way to get a car over to where Garth had fallen from his horse.

They both hiked the trail for two miles, where they found Garth's friend Will, pacing back and forth.

Garth lay flat on his back in the damp grass, groaning in agony. His face covered in mud, he spit out dirt.

Zach crouched, wincing at the old man's painful groans. "We're going to get you out of here." He had no idea how, but he had to try. Garth would be too heavy for the three of them to carry down the slope, and Zach was certain that Will's back would be out by the time they made it to his Land Rover. He turned, looking around for a cord of some sort, and then noticed the leather strap on Will's horse.

"Can we use your cord?" he asked Will, who paced to his horse and instantly returned with the cord.

Noah leaned in. "What's the plan?"

"We're going to use this leather strap..."

"To hoist him up into the saddle?" Noah finished for him.

"Exactly."

"Good thing my horse is gaited," Will said. "Perfect for that."

It was another fifteen minutes before both men helped Garth into Zach's car. Noah followed them to the hospital.Recognizing Zach from his previous visit to help George, and with Garth vouching for him, the hospital staff quickly accepted him as the attending physician.

After reviewing the X-rays, Zach determined that Garth had had a concussion and had dislocated his shoulder. He performed a closed reduction procedure, putting the ball of his upper arm back into the socket. The man would be wearing a sling for a few weeks until his shoulder was back in place, which meant that he would not be able to treat people for the next twelve to sixteen weeks until he got better.

And just like that, Zach's plans for his stay in Eron changed.

With Dr. Cami gone the next day, Zach had no choice but to fill in. The staff was thrilled to have the hospital founder's grandson temporarily take over the practice.

The next morning, his day started at seven am with a heart attack patient, then on to patching up another man who'd busted his lips when he fell down the stairs. Zach saw flu patients, treated a young man who'd overdosed on drugs, then helped a three-year-old who had shoved Legos into her nose, not to mention the three emergency procedures he performed that same day.

Zach felt like he was back on the mission field, where they had a limited number of doctors to treat a multitude of patients.

As busy as he was, he couldn't stop thinking about George's back pain, which is why he scheduled a procedure for him two days after becoming Eron's temporary doctor.

Throwing the mask in the trash can of the small doctor's room, Zach turned to the sink to rinse his face. After several hours of concentration on the spine, he was sweating profusely, but he also knew that Chloe and her family were anxiously waiting to hear how the procedure had gone.

The minute he stepped out to the waiting area, Chloe rose to her feet, and so did the rest of her family, except for Cynthia who stayed still in her wheelchair. Noah and his family were present, too.

Zach smiled. "Everything went very well, as expected." He reminded them that George was still sedated, but one person at a time could go in and see him. Then he began explaining about therapy and other things that would help George's recovery process.

Chloe threw her arms around him before he could finish whatever he was saying. "Thank you, Zach," she whispered.

Her hair smelled so good as it tickled his neck. Without thinking, Zach returned the embrace, his hands finding their way around her slender frame to caress her back.

"Now we pray and hope that he doesn't have any side effects," he said.

She stepped out of the embrace, then pulled up on tiptoes and unexpectedly planted her warm lips on his cheek, so warm that they heated up his blood. "Yes, we'll pray."

She turned, and only then did Zach remember that he and Chloe were not the only ones in the room. He rubbed a hand over his forehead, and he didn't have to look in the mirror to know that his face was extremely red.

There was something that went beyond chemistry between Zach and Chloe. More so, the attraction between them continued to spark like summer lightning.

CHAPTER 10

If only Chloe could say that she would never have to move again, now would be a great time to make that declaration. Unfortunately, the house she was moving into was a rental, which meant she would one day have to move again.

The owner of the house had recently relocated to a nursing home, and wanted to keep the house in her family instead of selling. For that reason, Chloe got a great deal. The only payment Chloe would make was the property tax fees.

She ran tape across the top of the final box in the living room. Her friends Sofia and Jules had helped her box the items over the last two days. Otherwise, she would be sweating over the anxiety of packing.

Even with her dad's recent procedure, Chloe had not pushed up her moving date, since George was recovering well.

Zach sent text messages daily to check on him. He'd also stopped by a couple of times during his lunch break to see how Chloe's dad was faring.

It was hard to think of Zach's name without feeling all mushy inside or smiling. When she'd kissed his cheek at the hospital, she had meant it to be friendly...maybe? Or at least that's what she'd told Noah and Cynthia when they thought it was a romantic gesture. The small peck had actually left her wondering and imagining what kissing Zach for real would be like.

She shook her head and kicked the box to the side. Noah was giving up an hour of his morning to come and help her move. He was the right man for her, and she wanted to give him a chance, but it was time for her to be honest with herself and him, even if he would be hurt if she told him how she felt. Hurting Noah was the last thing she wanted to do.

The only furniture she was moving out of the house were a couple of book shelves, since she'd ordered her bed and three other pieces of furniture from Ikea to be delivered to her new house today.

When the doorbell rang, she blinked and stared at the antique clock on the wall. It was only seven, and Noah wasn't supposed to arrive until eight thirty with two other guys.

She swung open the door to a husky man with more tattoos on his arm than she'd ever seen before. Her face wrinkled, her confusion increasing when she spotted a moving truck parked on the gravel.

"Hi." The man's greeting brought her gaze back to him. "We're here to move Chloe Love?"

"Uh… that's me, but I don't remember…"

"Zach Eron hired us," the man interrupted before she could finish her sentence.

She smiled and shook her head. *Zach.* He was probably getting ready to go to work, since the hospital kept him busy these days. "I really don't need that big of a truck. I don't have that many things."

"He said that you might say that. That's why he's on his way…"

Chloe didn't hear the rest of the man's words when the sound of tires crunching on the gravel drive caused her to raise her head. She watched the beige Land Rover scatter gravel as Zach parked next to the moving truck.

"That would be him right there." She pointed her chin in Zach's direction before facing the man. "Would you like some coffee?"

He politely declined and went to get his colleague from the truck.

Chloe sauntered to meet Zach in the driveway. She winced when her foot sank into a water puddle, soaking one of her slippers.

Zach grinned from ear to ear when he saw her. He held a box in his hands. Something edible, she hoped, since she was starving.

"Morning, Princess!" He gave her a once over, and Chloe wrapped her arms around her chest to shield herself from the crisp morning air. "I come bearing gifts."

Chloe smiled softly. "I can see that," she said in a soft tone. "I also see that you rented a humongous truck."

He shrugged a shoulder. "Since I don't own a truck, and I wanted to help, I thought that hiring the experts would get things done on time."

With his busy schedule at work, Chloe was surprised that he remembered her moving day from almost ten days ago when she'd told him. "I don't have a ton of things."

"Good grief, Chloe, are you really going to argue with me this early in the morning? Whether you have two or three boxes, I already paid the guys."

Perhaps this would save Noah's time, so he could get to work instead of moving her.

"Donuts and pastries?" He held the box out to her. "I brought enough to share with the movers."

She motioned for him to follow her into the house. "I'm starving."

Several minutes later, they sat at the dining table enjoying coffee and donuts. Jeanie smiled as she listened to Zach share how going through things in his house had helped him get a glimpse into his dad's side of the family. He also talked about the clay vase that he and Chloe had found downstairs.

"Silly me, I have this vase in my hand, and it seemed to emanate with spices of some sort. The moment I bring it to my nose to sniff, Chloe tells me that it had ashes that belonged to one of the family members." He lifted his hands to his head and wrinkled his nose. "My mind went 'Gross!" and I dropped the vase without even thinking. When it shattered, all it had was dried flower petals."

Jeanie broke out in laughter so hard that she clutched her stomach.

Chloe laughed, too, when she remembered his facial expression at the thought that he'd had a dead person's ashes right next to his face.

"And guess who did the cleaning?" she said between chuckles.

Zach's eyes sparkled and he elbowed her gently. "I was going to clean up, but you didn't leave me a choice."

Chloe was distracted when two burly guys trundled out through the front door, carrying boxes. She pushed back her chair. "I better go and make sure that they don't ruin my books."

Zach tugged at the hem of her sweater to pull her back. "The books are unbreakable. Let the guys do their job."

"Zach's right," Jeanie said, taking a sip of coffee from her mug.

When Cynthia emerged, maneuvering her wheelchair towards them, Zach's smile vanished and his gaze lowered. He flipped open the box of donuts on the table. "I brought some donuts, Cynthia."

Cynthia pushed a button on her chair to elevate herself a little so she would be at the same height as everyone else. She then stared at Zach with an unreadable expression before shifting her gaze to the donuts. "What kind of doctor encourages people to eat junk food?"

Chloe's stomach tied in knots as anger crept up in her heart. She could put up with a lot of things, but she was done putting up with Cynthia's harsh treatment of Zach. She was about to let out a piece of her mind when Cynthia pointed at one of the glazed donuts. "I like the one with blue icing."

Chloe reached for Zach's hand under the table and squeezed it. She savored his warmth and his presence.

"Don't you have to be at work, anyway?" Cynthia asked dismissively.

"I took today off so I could help Chloe with the move."

Chloe's eyes widened in surprise.

Cynthia shook her head, a ghost of a smile on her face. "You're full of surprises." She reached for the donut and took a huge bite.

"So are you, my child," Jeanie spoke to Cynthia. The way Zach had made the effort to check on George often since the procedure, Cynthia was probably getting used to his kindness and appearances at the house.

He took the day off for me? Chloe reached for her phone to text Noah, unsure how he would react to the cancellation. "Excuse me. I need to send a text to my helpers and let them know that they will not be needed."

Zach chatted with Jeanie while Chloe typed her text. When she was done, she pushed her chair back just as the movers angled an oak bookshelf through the door. "I need to get ready and get to the house before the movers get there."

Zach pulled up. "I'm coming with…"

Chloe narrowed her gaze. "How is it possible that you took the day off when you're Eron's only doctor?"

That heart melting smile appeared again. "Thanks to the beauty of the internet, I looked up doctors who travel like me, particularly those who are on standby for a day, a week, or however long you need them."

Overwhelmed by his generosity, her lips parted. "I can't believe that you took the day off just to help me move."

She knew that he didn't help her for pay back, but again, spending another day with Zach only meant that she would be getting more attached to him. Jeanie was watching her closely, perhaps waiting for her response.

"You can follow me," Chloe told Zach, since he didn't know her new address.

Two hours later, her furniture had been delivered and everything moved into the house. Noah had shown up in spite of her text, and insisted on helping the movers carry the boxes into the house, his way to pitch in before he left for work.

When Chloe had asked Zach to help her assemble the bed while they waited for the movers to arrive, he'd gotten frustrated at scrambling after the small pieces and ended up asking the movers to help set it up.

CHOICES

The two men had been glad to do the job, since they admitted they'd felt overpaid for transporting half a truck. "Easiest move ever," the tattooed guy had insisted.

Chloe stood in the empty ranch style house that smelled of fresh paint. The first place to herself! She'd always had roommates in design school; even as an adult in Boston she wouldn't have been able to save any money if she'd had to pay full rent by herself.

The three bedroom house had an open floor plan, which would give Chloe the space she needed for her drawing and sewing projects. She had gotten rid of the wallpaper and replaced it with light gray paint, after getting approval from the house owner.

She left the living room and walked through the hallway to her bedroom. As she unpacked the boxes with hangers, she heard frustrated sighs and groans coming from the room across the hall.

Zach was mounting the shelves in her project room, so she sauntered to the room across and poked her head through the open door. Zach sat on the floor hunched over a slab of wood, screwdriver in hand, his tongue sticking out in concentration, if his frown was any indication.

"You okay?"

The screwdriver fell out of his hand and thudded to the floor when he lifted his head. "Not really." He stared at the array of boards scattered all over the floor before returning his gaze to her. "I will be, as soon as I can get three of these shelves added to this." He gestured to the board in his hand. "Your project room needs to be ready before this day comes to an end." He picked up the screwdriver and resumed his work.

She didn't want him to stress over her projects on his one day off from the hospital. "Noah can stop by tomorrow and help assemble the shelves."

He took his eyes off his project and stared at her. "If it takes me all night to get this shelf mounted, I'm going to finish what I started." His jaw twitched a little as he turned his gaze back to the board in his hand. "If I can't get it done by tonight, then we can have Superman finish the job."

Superman? If she wasn't mistaken, Chloe had sensed an edge in the last words he said. Was he jealous of Noah? If only Zach knew how much he affected her.

She blinked and stared at the scattered papers on the floor. She hated reading manuals, but she stepped inside the room and picked up the papers, hoping that Zach could put them to good use. She held them out to him. "Maybe you can use this."

He stared at the papers in her hand and then at her. "I read so many books to research patients' diagnoses, that I would rather not read anything else if I can help it."

Yet he'd read the book she recommended, 'To Kill a Mockingbird.'

Chloe smiled at his confession. "Glad that I'm not the only one who finds manuals tedious."

A smile played at the corners of his mouth and he said, "Well, then, you better go get your bedroom set up, and I'll get back to my work. Last thing I need is for you to fire me."

She smiled and picked up a board from the floor. "Maybe if we work together, we'll be less likely to grow weary along the process of figuring things out."

He grinned and nodded slowly. "Two are always better than one."

"I will go get my phone, in case we need YouTube as our back up." She set the board on the floor and left to fetch her purse, returning in a few minutes.

They worked well as a team, and the time passed quickly with him sharing his funny experiences of treating the residents of Eron. He also talked about treating an injured deer that one of the residents had called him about after suddenly running into it with his motorcycle.

With the help of a short DIY video on YouTube, they had all eight shelves mounted to the wall in no time. Well, perhaps it was more time, but it was hard for Chloe to keep track of time when she was with Zach.

After the shelves were done, Chloe emptied the boxes of clothes in her room while Zach helped set up the TV. They worked together to unpack the books and videos from the boxes. Neither had paid attention to the time until Chloe's stomach complained with a loud growl.

"Somebody's getting hungry!" Zach teased, and Chloe patted her stomach.

"You must be hungry, too, by now," she said. "I have no idea what time it is, but it's definitely past lunch time."

Zach patted his pockets. "I don't know where my phone is, but I think I could use something to eat."

Chloe felt terrible for having forgotten to feed her guest. She rose from her spot on the carpet and went to the coffee table for her phone. "It's already four."

"It feels like noon to me." Exactly—not just because she was busy, but from enjoying his company. "I didn't plan ahead for dinner, but...maybe I should order a pizza. Will that be okay with you?"

He smiled. "I'm not picky. Pizza sounds good. No more desserts for me, since the town's people have baked me so many treats of all sorts every day that I've started turning them down."

Chloe gave him a scowl. "Zach Eron, you did not turn down a cheesecake, by any chance, did you?"

He chuckled. "Are you kidding me? If I got a cheesecake, you would be the first to know, because I can't think of a cheesecake without you coming to mind." His face heated when his words registered, and he quickly looked back at the book in his hand.

"The Art of Fashion," he read the title and flipped through a few pages before he tucked it on the book shelf. He reached for another book. "King Arthur." He held the book up to Chloe. "Have you seen the movie?"

Her lips parted in surprise. "I didn't even know that they made a movie out of it."

"That's one of the few fiction books I would have enjoyed, but I never read the entire book," Zach said. "When I misplaced the book, I never got around to replacing it."

"King Arthur is another one of my all-time favorite reads," Chloe admitted.

"All the more reason for you to watch the movie sometime."

"Books are always better than the movies, you know."

"I guess I'll have to borrow your book, so I can refresh my memory."

After he set the book on the shelf, she gestured him to the couch. They'd had a long day. "Why don't you leave everything and come have a break. I will get you some water, and then order us a pizza."

He stared at the mound of books on the floor, then the movies they'd arranged on the shelf. "Maybe we can watch one of these movies."

A movie and pizza sounded relaxing, and she definitely owed Zach for having worked him hard without feeding him lunch. She walked back to him, doubting she had a movie for him worth watching. Netflix would be a worthwhile investment, but Chloe rarely had the time to watch TV. "Did you see anything that caught your attention?"

He kept a steady gaze on the row of DVDs. "I've never seen so many documentaries in my whole life."

Chloe pulled out a nature movie and handed it to him. "This is not a documentary."

He read the cover. "Ocean Creatures." He gave her a look. "Um, lets see if there's anything else."

He shoved the video back in the stack, then tapped his finger on the row of DVDs as he scanned his options. He pulled out another DVD. "African Cats." He held the DVD out to her. "What do you think?"

It had been a while since she saw any of the movies she had, and she didn't care what they did or watched as long as he was there. "That sounds good."

"I'll keep shelving your books until the pizza gets here," he said. "As long as you don't add olives or okra to my pizza."

"What happened to not being picky?" she asked as she looked up the number to the local pizza diner.

He scratched his jaw. "I guess I have a few things I can live without."

The doorbell rang as Chloe waited for the diner to answer her call. With her phone on her ear, she went to answer the door. She blinked at the setting sun on the horizon.

"Happy moving day!"

Chloe took the phone off her ear and hung up to greet her senior friends.

In their mid-seventies, both had a big brown bag with a wafting scent of something savory.

"Hi, Patty." She then turned to greet Patty's husband, whose smile met his eyes. "Hi, Jim!"

"We thought you could use some dinner," Jim said.

Chloe opened the door wide. "Come in. Thanks for bringing dinner. It smells like pizza," she said, although it was hard to identify the aroma combined with Patty's perfume and cigarette breath.

"Guess what the hungry bear said?" Jim chuckled before Chloe could respond, which caused Chloe to burst out laughing, too. Something she did whenever she was with the steely-eyed man, whose laughter had turned into wheezing. The man doubled over in a fit of coughing, then grabbed at his back. "Oh, oh, my back!"

"Come on, Jimmy, let's hold off on the jokes until we sit down," Patty said in a raspy voice, obviously unconcerned for her husband's plight. To Chloe, she said, "We brought you some calzones from Riccis."

Chloe put her hand to her chest, letting her laughter subside before she spoke. "That's so thoughtful of you."

As they headed to the kitchen, Zach paused from his work and flashed the older couple a grin. He'd met Patty and Jim on Bingo night.

"Hey, Dr. Eron!" Jim stretched his hand out to Zach cheerfully, and Zach rose to greet him.

"Listen to this, listen," Jim laughed and spoke to Zach. "The old man was sitting on the examining table in the doctor's office having his hearing checked. The doctor poked his light scope in the old man's ear and said, 'Hey, you have a suppository in your ear.' Guess what the old man said?"

Jim grinned, waiting for Zach's response, but Zach was obviously clueless. His eyes wide, Zach stammered, "Uh...um..."

"Rats, said the old man, now I know where my hearing aid went." The sound of Jim's laughter filled the house. Zach chuckled, and Chloe laughed so hard that her stomach hurt. It wasn't that Jim's jokes were funny, but the old man's laugh was infectious. His wife didn't join in, though–perhaps she'd laughed so much over the years that she was tired of doing it.

After spending an hour sharing laughter and meaty calzones, the older couple declined the invitation to stay and watch a movie with Zach and Chloe.

"Babysitting the grandkids tonight," Patty explained as they said their goodbyes.

Zach had plopped onto the lime green sofa, with his feet propped up contentedly on the coffee table and his arm draped carelessly over the backrest. Chloe sat on the other end of the couch as the narrator on the DVD discussed the life of an African lion.

Although the cozy scenario should be alarming, Chloe didn't give a thought to anything or anybody else except for the man sitting a few inches from her.

CHAPTER 11

The next morning, Chloe woke to the sound of the doorbell and light streaming through the window. Throwing on her robe, she staggered to the front door only to find Noah standing doe-eyed with a bouquet of red roses in one hand and a Styrofoam cup in the other.

"Sorry to show up so early. I felt bad that I worked late last night, and didn't return to help you unpack," he said. "If you have any work left to do, I can come back this afternoon, since I get off early today."

She didn't feel it necessary to tell him that Zach had stayed and helped the entire time, so she used the easier response. "The guys who moved stuff helped set up most of the furniture." That was mostly the truth.

She ran a hand over her groggy face. "Want to come in?"

He studied her for a moment, then handed her the cup. "I brought you a latte." He then handed her the flowers. "I better let you get ready."

"Thank you so much for the flowers!" *You didn't have to do this.* He made it harder for her to be honest with him when he was this nice.

Once he left, she got ready for work and was at her shop by nine-thirty. After she and Jules had gone through the excel spreadsheet of the previous days' sales, her assistant bombarded her with questions about Zach.

"Did Hottie stay for the entire day?"

"Yes."

"What did you feed him?"

"Calzones from Ricci's."

"Please tell me that you kissed at some point."

It wouldn't have been a bad idea. "I have to finalize things with Noah before I cross that line."

Jules gave her an eye roll, and Chloe put her computer to sleep before closing it.

"Does Sweet Pea know that Zach spent an entire day with you?"

"No." Chloe set her focus on the glass jewelry counter.

She blinked when she noticed that one of their most expensive collector rings was not on the shelf. Its absence was obvious because nobody had bought it from the time she started her boutique. Chloe frowned and turned to Jules, who was leaning forward on the counter. "Did you finally sell the star ring?" Of course she hadn't, since it wasn't listed in the sales they'd just gone through.

Jules' forehead wrinkled and her eyes flew to the glass case. "What? No, I didn't!" She gave the display another cursory scan. "Oh my gosh, I don't see the Faith Diamond, either!"

Chloe's chest tightened with fear as she fought to stay calm. The ring was worth $40,000.

She had worn the Faith Diamond at an auction of one-of-a-kind jewelry when she'd visited a fashion house in Italy four years ago. Afterwards, she'd kept it on display, hoping that one day her boutique would draw in the right person to buy the pendant. Speechless, she massaged her temple.

Jules threw both hands over her tight hair bun. "I had my key the entire time, and I doubt anybody came behind the counter besides me."

Chloe paced back and forth, wondering how someone had gotten into the jewelry case without breaking it. She and Jules had grown up together. Although Jules was wild in some ways, being a thief was one thing Chloe knew her friend wasn't. Of course, they had been apart for almost thirteen years. Was it possible Jules had changed during that time? *No, she couldn't.*

"I know it looks like I stole those items," Jules said, probably suspecting what was going on in Chloe's mind. "But I...I even saw those pieces before I left to grab a coffee at three pm."

"Jules," Chloe said firmly. "You're a lot of things, but a thief is not one of them."

Jules let out a sigh of relief. Chloe moved to her project room to call Sofia, whose office was upstairs. She then examined both the front and back doors for any signs of forced entry, but found nothing. Someone had the key to their store and their jewelry case. *That was odd.*

"We need to call Trevor," Sofia suggested once Jules filled her in on the details of what had happened.

"Hi, honey." Sofia kept a hand laid on her forehead as she spoke on the phone to her fiancé, who was also the town's detective. "Could you please come by the boutique ASAP? Chloe's shop has been robbed."

Minutes later, the wail of a siren died outside the shop, followed by the door's abrupt opening to announce the tall, dark-skinned man.

"I came as fast as I could." Trevor adjusted the gun on his hip, and Sofia greeted him by planting a soft kiss on his lips.

When Sofia stepped aside, Trevor tilted his chin to Chloe and Jules. "Jules, can I ask you a few questions in private?"

Jules eyes widened and she pointed a finger to her chest. "You think I stole the jewelry?"

Trevor shook his head. "That's not what I said..."

"Then I have nothing to hide." Jules crossed her arms over her chest, her mouth tight. "Whatever you're going to ask me, you can ask in front of Chloe and Sofia."

Trevor let out a slow sigh, as if was dreading his next words. "Hank has been taken in to the station for questioning."

Jules gasped, Sofia blinked, and Chloe's hand flew to her mouth.

"After money went missing from four other businesses within the last two weeks, the puzzle was easy to put together, since he was connected to all those businesses in one way or another. We installed cameras in those places." He gritted his teeth. "I should've consulted you first, before we installed cameras in your building too, but once I found out his felony record, It was best to not involve you guys. I hate to say that he can't deny…"

"You've never given him the chance." Jules' voice rose and she pointed a finger at Trevor as her fear turned to anger. "You've always wanted something to accuse him of, ever since you laid eyes on him."

"Jules," Sofia stepped between her cousin and her fiancé and tried to grab Jules' hand. "It's not exactly like that…"

"Leave me alone!" Jules snapped and tossed Sofia's hand to the side. Her eyes narrowed. "He didn't do it!" She turned and ran to the back, all the way to Chloe's project room, yelling again, "He didn't do it!" She barreled into the room and slammed the door with a final click.

They all went silent for a few seconds. Finally, Trevor told Chloe and Sofia that Hank was wanted in Woodland Park, a city fifty miles south of Eron, where he'd been involved in an illegal drug deal. "I will get your jewelry back to you as soon as we settle the case."

After Trevor left, Chloe and Sofia went to the room Jules had locked herself in and knocked.

"Jules, can you please open the door?" Sofia said.

"Go away! You all think you're so perfect," Jules snarled. "I don't even want to be a part of your stupid wedding. You're gonna have to find someone else to take my place."

Chloe stared at Sofia's reddening face. Poor Sofia was no doubt hurt, since she was trying so hard to reconnect with her family members. "She doesn't mean it," Chloe whispered.

"I don't care if you're not a part of my wedding!" Sofia shot back.

Jules and Sofia exchanged a few more sharp words. Chloe popped her knuckles, wondering how to calm this storm. Finally, she took a deep breath and spoke up, "Stop! Both of you."

Thankfully it worked. Silence settled immediately, and Chloe winced, "I don't mean to yell. Sorry."

Sofia let out a shuddering breath and gave an understanding look before she turned to leave.

Chloe inched towards the door and rested her forehead there, her heart drumming with tension. "Jules, you of all people know that we're not perfect..."

"Just leave me alone!" Jules voice was still high pitched. "Is that too much to ask?"

Fine. Chloe would save her pep talk for another time. She needed to have a mental break, too. She hated conflict, and tried to avoid it at all cost—for the most part.

She spent the rest of the day tending to customers who showed up while she battled with new unexpected trials that she hadn't seen coming when she'd started her day that morning.

During the afternoon lull with no customers, Chloe sat behind the cash register and popped her knuckles until they hurt. She then buried her head in her arms on the counter, doing what she should have done all along. "Lord, please give me peace of mind. How can I reconcile my friends when my own life is just as chaotic?" She was silent for a while as she thought through her prayer. Peace was what she needed, but how could she focus on praying for it when her mind was currently frenzied with all the things she needed to get done?

She sat up as the fashion show preparations roiled in her mind. She needed to follow up with vendors and volunteers. The seamstress, the tailor, the stage lighting crew...there were so many details to take care of, yet she felt no strength to do any of them at the moment. She could at least try to pursue peace and reconciliation.

Leaving her teenaged employee to tend to the shop, Chloe went upstairs to find Sofia. Thankfully, that conversation went well.

She hoped for the same results when she returned downstairs to knock on the door Jules was hiding behind.

"Come on, Jules, is it your intention to hide in there all day, or do you plan to emerge at some point?"

"If you think that I'm in here crying so you can have something to laugh about, then no! My tear ducts are too proud to cry."

What a complicated girl Jules was. Yet she was a good person, and a special friend—she just had deep wounds underneath. Chloe blew out a breath. "Why would you think that it would make me happy to see you cry?" Even though it would be sort of nice to see her shed a tear like a normal person for once. The girl was hard core, though deep down she had a heart of gold.

Chloe leaned her forehead on the door again and sighed. Maybe she could be more creative with her pep talk this time. "Remember how you and I used to feel sorry for ourselves because our moms never gave us the chance to meet our dads?" Jules was silent and Chloe continued. "Yet God helped both of us, and gave us wonderful step dads. I was always jealous of you for at least having a mom who cared enough about you to drag you along on all her unstable moves. Me, on the other hand—I wondered why my mom left me behind, why she didn't take me like your mom did." Now she understood that Cynthia had been young, and was actually grateful she'd left her with Jeanie instead.

"You should be glad that your mom was smart enough to leave you in one place." Jules words came out faltering. "That's why you turned out normal."

Chloe chuckled. At least she was talking. "You think so? I guess you haven't noticed that I'm a coward."

"Says the girl who breaks up fights with fierce men." Jules' voice sounded as if there was a smile in there.

"And who tackled Dexter Boone in junior high when he said I sounded like a loser for attending the senior's bake sale instead of going to the fall dance with him?"

"He had it coming."

Jules had always been protective of Chloe, and was ready to jump at anybody's throat if they said anything mean to Chloe. The two girls had been inseparable. While Jules was always ready to throw the first punch, Chloe's job had been to make amends on behalf of Jules' actions. It had crushed Chloe's heart when Jules' mom decided to leave Eron, taking Jules with her, during their second year of junior high. Despite their distance apart, they'd found a way to keep in touch by email, calling, or texting.

"You know what I mean, Jules. I'm always playing peacemaker, to the point that I can't be honest, just because I'm afraid to hurt people's feelings." She let out a mirthless laugh. "I can't even tell Noah that I'm in love with Zach..." She trailed off, feeling vulnerable admitting her inner struggles. "I have major abandonment issues, Jules. That's why I admire you for always being honest." *Except for the times that honesty was brutal.*

"You're worse off than I thought," Jules said through the door. "We're quite a pair." Her next words were weak but hopeful. "And you still want me for a friend?"

"Always!"

"Whatever. I'm still not leaving this room until you and Sofia leave for the day." She spoke with finality, and Chloe knew Jules always meant what she said.

It was still two hours before closing time, and Chloe needed to force herself to go through her to-do lists and respond to her emails, so she could feel she'd been productive for the day.

While she waited for her laptop to reboot, her phone buzzed with an incoming text. Chloe welcomed the distraction. Her heart did a somersault when she saw the sender's name. *Zach.*

Heard about your friend's boyfriend going to jail. Is she okay?

Chloe hadn't known about the jail part yet, and for sure Jules didn't either, since she didn't have her phone with her to check social media.

Chloe typed her response, her heart feeling lighter. **I see that you've picked up on the town's enthusiasm for following social media.**

His response came instantly. **Interesting what I hear from my patients and the nurses. I get live stream, more detailed than social media. How are you holding up?**

Her fingers hesitated before she admitted, **Not too good. Jules is livid, and I just had to referee an argument between her and Sofia.**

Want me to come over? his next text offered.

No, you have to treat your patients.

He sent a tearful emoji and added, **Your friends are blessed to have you, everything's gonna be alright.**

She hoped so, and really soon. Last thing she needed was to have her friends leave town again. Not Sofia, since she was getting married, but Jules didn't have a strong reason to stay in Eron.

Once Sofia left for the day, Chloe decided to do the same. She hung the *We're Closed* sign on the front of the door, then shut it. Grabbing her handbag, she stepped out through the back door and closed it behind her.

When she turned, she spotted a familiar lean figure in dark jeans and a button up blue shirt strolling through the sparse parking lot towards her. Only because it was Zach did she manage a half smile in return when he smiled at her. She didn't feel like smiling. She allowed her shoulders to sag, almost dropping her purse to the ground.

Zach jogged the remaining short distance to the sidewalk where she stood. "You okay?" He brushed a loose curl of hair from her forehead and gently tucked it behind her ear.

Her knees felt weak, and she shook her head, keeping her gaze down lest she drown in his eyes and did something foolish. Like staring at his lips hungrily, or worse yet, kissing him.

She was glad he couldn't read her mind. His strong arms wrapped her in an embrace, his chin rested on her head and Chloe inhaled the clean reassuring scent of him. She tried not to think of the fight between her friends, or the look of confusion, fear, and betrayal she'd seen in Jules' eyes before she'd sped to the back room. Instead, she allowed herself to be comforted by Zach's warmth, feeling safe and vulnerable as all the day's tension slowly drained away.

After what seemed like several seconds in his arms, she was disappointed when Zach stepped back. He took the purse from her hand, then offered her his elbow. She slid her hand through the crook of his warm arm.

"I want to hear all about your day over dinner, and then we should go see a movie afterwards...a real movie in the theater this time, not a documentary."

She chuckled, and elbowed him, as they started walking towards the parking lot. "I have real movies. Remember we watched one yesterday?"

"It was narrated, which to me is considered a documentary." He winked at her. "But then, who am I to argue with a princess?"

He dropped her hand when they neared his car, which was parked nearer than Chloe's vehicle. "Lets drive my car. We'll come back for your Altima after the movie."

Even if there were a few prying eyes of business owners closing their stores for the day, and a few people walking on the sidewalk, Chloe decided not to worry about what would be said about her and Zach on social media. In fact, this one time, she didn't care what anyone might think, except maybe Noah. Maybe by tomorrow she would have gathered enough nerve to tell Noah that things weren't going to work out between them.

She instantly shoved Noah to the back of her mind when Zach reminded her to buckle her seat belt before he fired the engine. She fastened her seat belt, then glanced up at him and smiled.

He smiled back and reached for Chloe's hand, entwining his warm fingers with hers, not letting go as he drove them toward some unknown restaurant, since they had not discussed where to eat.

That was fine with her, because all she cared about was the man she was with.

CHAPTER 12

The smell of fresh air after the rain was one of those things Zach would never get tired of breathing. He took another inhalation of the spring air as he approached the metal building which housed the town's ice skating rink.

After another long week at work, Zach had decided to go ice-skating. Losing a patient earlier that day was a good reason he didn't want to go home to solitude. He needed to do something relaxing.

In his profession, Zach had seen plenty of deaths in people of all ages and types, but somehow, he found himself unable to stop thinking of his last patient this afternoon.

Zach loved elderly people, and his patient had been in her late seventies. She and her husband had been just passing through Eron when she'd been brought in. The woman had clearly had a heart attack, and although she showed no vital signs, Zach had tried his hardest, applying compressions far longer than required. But it was too late, and he'd been unable to revive her.

The husband's loud wails when Zach told him that his wife's life couldn't be saved had pierced Zach's heart. Maybe Chloe's soft spot for the elderly was starting to rub off on him, too.

It was hard to believe that April was already here. Time was going way faster than he wanted it to. He hadn't anticipated enjoying the small town as much as he was right now, but he knew who was behind his enjoyment—the African American princess.

Zach hadn't seen Chloe since last week when he'd picked her up at her boutique. He'd been intrigued listening to her problems and cries of concern. He'd mostly enjoyed being the one to make her laugh after she'd had a long day at work. Thankfully, she had texted him that things were back to normal with her friend Jules.

His phone vibrated just as he was reaching for the handle of the heavy metal door. He stepped aside and pulled the phone from his leather jacket. It was his mom, Monique, calling.

"Zach, honey, are you still alive and kicking in that town?"

He had told her when she called him the first few days in town that he doubted he would last here longer than a month, since he missed the beach. Thanks to Chloe, he was now hesitant to leave. "I'm starting to like this town, actually."

"Looks like I won't be able to see you until I come to your friend's fashion show."

Zach realized he hadn't told his family of his new role in town. "I'm now the town's doctor, ever since their only doctor got hurt. At least until he recovers." That's why he stopped by Garth's house whenever he could, to make sure Garth kept up with his physical therapy so he could return to work and release Zach.

"I hope you can still come home before you take off for New Zealand."

Of that, he had no idea, so he chose to keep silent.

"Anyway," Monique continued. "Addie told me about your designer friend. She probably had a lot to do with the candles you sent for my birthday."

"Guilty as charged." Zach grinned as if he were face to face with his mom instead of talking to her on the phone. "I got the jewelry from her shop, and she insisted I add more personal gifts to your package."

"I loved the honeysuckle candles the most." Chloe's favorite, as well. "So, tell me about this Chloe. What is she like?"

Zach rubbed his forehead and thought of the many different ways he could describe Chloe Love. Memories of their last time together resurfaced–a week ago, when he'd taken her to dinner after she'd had a rough day. He smiled when he remembered that he'd made her smile, and how she had laughed with him while they watched a comedy at the theater.

He cleared his throat before he spoke. "She's kind. When she smiles, you feel warm. She cares about others." Even her mom, who seemed unlovable. It had warmed Zach's heart to see Chloe ready to stand up to her mom when she thought that Cynthia was about to throw her mean remarks at Zach.

"I'm listening." Mom's voice pulled him back to their conversation, and Zach cleared his throat again.

"She's very passionate about anything she puts her efforts into. Fashion, mostly, but she also has a special place in her heart for elderly people. You'll like her Mom. There's no way you could interact with her and not see…"

"I already like her," Monique interrupted before Zach could finish all the things he wanted to tell her about Chloe. "I think you've found your far-away princess, after all. I'm not a praying person, but it's always been my heart's desire for you and Addie to find that special someone."

Zach nodded as if his mom could see him. *The far-away princess, indeed.* Odd that his mom still remembered that. Based on Chloe's conversations, when she spoke about Noah, she made it seem like they were good friends who were still figuring out how to define their friendship. Zach already knew what he wanted from Chloe—he wanted more than friendship from her, and he was certain that Chloe felt the same way. He let out a sigh when he thought of where his relationship with Chloe stood. "It's complicated right now."

"Love can do anything."

Zach could only hope his mom was right. After hanging up with his mom, with a promise to see her in just over a month, Zach swung open the metal door to the room filled with disco lights.

After paying his skate fee to a girl with a pierced nose, he was directed to another booth where he could rent or buy skates.

He tried to ignore the odor of feet mixed with stale pizza as he thought of his mom's words about love doing anything.

His mom of all people had never been a good example of a stable relationship, since she had never been married. She'd gotten pregnant by Zach's dad, and Zach was almost positive that by the time his dad died, Mom was not involved with him anymore. Then there was Addie's dad, who was another famous actor she'd dated for less than a year, and things had never worked out between them, although Addie was conceived in the process. Still, Monique was a good mom, in the best way, and Zach was grateful for that. She always took care of him and Addie, and made time, especially recently as she got older, to stay on top of what was going on in Zach and Addie's lives.

Once he'd gotten his skates, Zach toted them to the concession area to lace them up. He'd just put on his leather gloves when he spotted Chloe.

She was always a breath of fresh air. It was almost as if her fragrance reached him across the distance, mostly because he didn't have to be standing next to her to know how fresh and delightful she smelled.

The rink's neon lights that could trigger a seizure in someone more sensitive made it hard to make out the color of her long sweater.

Chloe brushed back a strand of her hair while she spoke with the young man running the skates booth. Was she going to skate? Zach's heart did a happy dance as he waited on the bench.

Slow skating music echoed in the background, luring a few teenagers and young adults onto the ice. Zach turned back to Chloe. When she left the booth with no skates, Zach jolted from the bench to meet her as she neared.

"Chloe!" he hollered, startling her and causing her to drop her purse. Zach picked it up and held her hand.

"Zach." She stared at him up and down. "Are you okay?" She ran a hand over his shoulder, her face expressing concern. "I'm so sorry that your patient did not make it."

She'd been the first person he texted when the woman died, asking for prayers for the woman's husband.

"It happens all the time." Yet this time had been different. "Come with me to the rink," he said instead, not wanting to talk about work or his day.

She stared at him in disbelief, as if he'd asked a hard task.

"Please." *Did you have to add a plea?* Yes, he did – this was Chloe, and he wanted to spend every available moment he still had in town with her. If he didn't, Noah would do just that. Yes, a plea was necessary in this matter.

"I don't skate. The only reason I came here was to talk to the guy who will be doing the stage lights for the fashion show."

When Zach had told her that Noah was fixing the house on his property for her fashion show, she'd jumped up and down in excitement, thanking him repeatedly. Although she was still giving him a hard time by insisting on paying her share for the remodel.

He returned to the present and asked, "Will this be your first time on ice?"

"Oh, no." she said, shaking her head, " It's just been a long time, way too long."

"You need a refresher course."

She reluctantly turned with him to head back to the shoe rental booth. Once she'd laced her skates, she pulled her knitted green hat and gloves from her purse before locking her handbag in a locker behind the skate booth.

Zach offered her his elbow and they slowly made their way to the outside of the rink, where the beginner skaters were. They glided around the rink, giving him a chance to ask her something that had been bugging him. "Why Love?"

She paused and blinked in surprise at his question.

Zach clarified, "I mean, why is your last name Love? Yet your grandma has a different last name?"

He had to lean in a little too close to her to hear her words over the music, and he felt himself blushing.

She raised her voice a little. "My grandma chose that name for me. She wanted it to be a meaningful reminder that I'm loved even if I didn't have a mom or dad, that it doesn't take a biological parent to feel loved. But more importantly, to know that I have a heavenly Father who saw me and knew me before I was born... that my life wasn't a mistake."

"Your grandma sounds like a very wise person in my book," Zach said. "The name Love suits your personality."

"Thanks," she breathed, and smiled before skating away to the center where the rest of the experienced skaters were.

So she knew how to skate after all. Zach skated and circled around a group of teenage boys and girls to get to Chloe. When he caught up to her, he took a deep breath and spoke. "Looks like you haven't lost your touch."

Her eyes sparkled and her smile crinkled the corners of her eyes as she took an imaginary bow. "Thanks for the refresher course."

He held out his hand. "May I join you, please?"

She took his hand without hesitation, and he felt the tension even through the gloves they both wore. They fell into each other's rhythm immediately as they circled around the rink.

"When was the last time you've been on ice?" he asked.

"I was thirteen. Then life got too busy, and skating was one of those things I had to cancel out of my schedule."

Zach smiled. "You seem to be a natural."

She wrinkled her nose. "I don't think so. How about you? You're pretty good at it for someone who grew up in a place without snow."

"It's from taking advantage of places like this, and whenever I travel to places that encourage the sport. I spent a winter in Russia and worked with this doctor who loved skating. We did a lot of that whenever we had time."

"During your adult life, have you ever stayed in one place for longer than one year?"

He hesitated, but she kept staring at him, waiting for the response she so deserved to know before she got entangled with him.

"No," he finally admitted. Travelling was a calling for Zach, one he felt God wanted him to do, at least for now, and he didn't have any regrets.

When a fast paced song came on, Zach picked up his pace slightly, and Chloe matched him. They went faster and faster, hands clinging, faces cold, and he smiled when he heard her delighted laugh.

Zach lost count of how many times they circled the rink, and forgot about the fact that he should be bored in this town, because he was anything but. There was something carefree about skating with Chloe.

Finally, he tugged her hand gently to slow her, then more firmly to bring her around to face him.

Chloe's eyes were bright, her teeth chattering as she grinned up at him. "Oh, I forgot how fun that can be. I feel like I'm thirteen again."

He smiled and touched a gloved finger to her nose. "You look cold."

"Maybe a little." She shrugged. "Aren't you cold?"

Nope, his whole body was warm, and she was definitely the reason for the sudden rise in his body temperature. "I'm okay."

Zach tightened his grip on her hand, pulling her closer. He tugged the glove of his free hand off with his teeth and tucked it under his arm, slipping his other arm around her waist. When he brushed a bare finger along the soft skin on her jaw, her eyes widened and her breath caught.

Staring at her rounded lips overrode his common sense. With no idea what he was doing, he dipped his head slightly, feeling her breath against his lips. *Don't do it!* came the small voice in the back of his mind.

She breathed his name.

"Chloe," he murmured. "You look beautiful."

Confusion flickered in her gaze, followed by something else that he couldn't identify. Oblivious to the skaters whizzing by them, and the clicks and flashes of a camera going off, neither of them moved away from the movement of his un-gloved fingers dancing back and forth along her soft lips, and then to her jaw. Her skin was soft, her lips even softer. Zach wondered what her lips would feel like under his.

"Will you just kiss her already?" A voice snapped them back to their audience as a teenage boy skated past them.

Applause followed as another flash went off.

Chloe shook her head and dropped Zach's hand as if washing free of him. "I have to go!"

She skated away, but Zach remained frozen for a moment longer, a bit jarred that he'd just touched her jaw and her lips, almost kissed her, even. If another moment had gone by of them staring at each other with intense longing, he might have wanted to do more than touch her lips.

Perhaps he could do just that. He skated off the ice to catch up to her, but she was nowhere in sight.

By the time he changed into his shoes to go search outside, she was already halfway across the parking lot. "Chloe, wait!"

She didn't turn, but kept walking, ignoring him. Zach jogged to catch up with her. "Are you mad at me?" It was either that, or she was as shaken up by their reaction as he was. "I don't want you to be upset."

She slowed her steps and turned to glare at him, the least scary glare he'd ever seen, but she wasn't smiling. Placing her hand on her hip, she spoke carefully. "I live in this town, and you don't care what people say about you because you're leaving," The sparkle in her eyes had vanished. "I really don't want us to be in a situation that draws more gossip for the town's social media page. I should never have agreed to skate in the first place."

"But you loved it!" And he'd enjoyed every moment on the ice with her, especially the time when he'd almost kissed her, until the town gossips interrupted their intimate moment. "Can't people in this town get a life instead of stalking everyone?"

She sighed, and moved her hand to clutch her gray handbag. "I really need to go," she said flatly, and turned.

"I'm sorry if I humiliated you." He had no idea why he was apologizing, but he didn't know what else to say to her.

She threw her arms up in frustration. "No need to apologize."

Then why are you mad at me? he felt like asking, but now was not the time.

That night, as Zach contemplated whether to go to bed or scroll through channels for late night TV shows, his phone buzzed from the coffee table and he picked it up. Hope resurfaced when Chloe's name displayed on the screen, signaling a text from her.

I'm sorry that I got mad at you for no apparent reason.

He smiled and typed his response. **No need to apologize. What happened?** He already knew but had to ask.

I just got carried away with the ice skating, I think.

He understood what she meant, because it had nothing to do with the sport at all. **Ice skating can do that to you.**

Forgive me?

Do I have any choice but to forgive the princess? He added a smiley emoji and hit Send.

It was a long time before Zach fell asleep, because he couldn't stop thinking of the lips he'd almost tasted today. Whether Chloe admitted it or not, there was definitely some kind of vibe in the air between them, and even though it couldn't be seen, it was very much felt—that vibe that made them gravitate towards each other.

CHAPTER 13

Latte in one hand, and a glass vase of red roses in the other, Noah Buzz walked the one block to Love's Boutique. He'd parked his car a couple of blocks from Chloe's shop, since he was adding shelving units in one of the shops on Main Street today.

The morning drizzle didn't help his mood. Despite the bright smiles and friendly waves from shop owners as they opened their doors for business, Noah struggled to force a smile back in response. He was about to lose the girl he'd worked so hard to have in his life—actually, he'd already lost her, the moment Zach stepped into their lives.

Even a fool could see that Chloe loved Zach more than anything. The way she swooned the moment he entered the room, it almost felt like she forgot everything around her but Zach. Whether Zach was leaving town or not, her heart belonged to the doctor.

Had she ever loved Noah? Deep down, he knew the answer. He'd always known, but had ignored the truth and kept trying to push his way into her heart. First by constantly asking her out until she had given in to their first date, then a second date three weeks later, and two other dates after that. Come to think of it, he was always the one initiating dates in the relationship.

Plenty of girls flirted with Noah all the time, but he didn't want any of those girls. He wanted Chloe Love.

Lord, am I asking too much? Are you punishing me for my rebellious youth? Not that God operated that way. He didn't do paybacks, but it was hard not to think of it that way.

He didn't have to see the 'We're Open' sign on the front door to know that the boutique was open. Chloe always opened her boutique thirty minutes early. He set the flowers on the ground and tugged on the knob to open the door. Holding the door open with his body, he crouched and picked up the flowers.

Like the day would go, his hope vanished when his eyes landed on Chloe's scowling associate, who had her hair tied in a pointy ponytail. Noah could only wonder how Jules ended up on the top of the list of Chloe's best friends. Only Chloe could see the best in everybody.

"Hi, Jules." He forced a smile, not expecting one in return.

Jules glanced at him briefly before returning to her phone, or whatever she was doing behind the counter. "You can leave your flowers here." She pointed her chin next to a bouquet of yellow, purple, and pink ranunculus in a glass vase. "As you can see, Zach already beat you to it."

Zach. Just that name stirred up a quiet roar of anxiousness deep inside him. He felt as if he had an enemy for life.

"You can keep the coffee, since Hottie already brought a coffee for Chloe." She then lifted a styrofoam cup. "For me, too. Plus, she will not be back for another hour or so."

So Zach's nickname was Hottie? What did they call Noah behind his back? He let out a slow breath. "Where's Chloe?"

She examined her painted fingernails. "I usually don't answer to anybody, especially if it has nothing to do with shop transactions." She then stared at him. "But if you must know, she and Hottie went to the seamstress. They're getting clothes picked up. As you know, the fashion show is just around the corner."

She took a sip of her drink and turned back to her phone.

Noah's sister had shown him a picture of Zach and Chloe at the ice-skating rink, and he'd ended up being upset with her for shoving each picture of Zach and Chloe in his face. Yet what he was really upset about was Zach – he was jealous to say the least.

Blood burning, Noah shut his eyes and ran a hand through his short hair. When he opened his eyes, Jules was leaning forward and resting her forearms on the counter, her eyes on him.

"It's guys like you I don't get." Her words caught his attention, "At what point are you going to realize that Chloe is not your girlfriend?"

Right. Painful reminder he already knew.

Jules was always abrasive, but Noah assumed her bluntness today had everything to do with her bruised ego from her boyfriend being in jail for stealing, and a few other charges from whichever town he'd come from.

"What do you mean?" He asked, even though he knew exactly what she meant.

"Sometimes the toughest call you can make is admitting when you're in over your head." She reached for her cup and sipped cooly. "You want to tell me that from the beginning of your relationship with Chloe, even before Hottie showed up in town, that she loved you as much as you love her?"

Silence. Of course Chloe loved him, or liked him—what was the difference?

"If you think you're in love with Chloe, then you need to let her go," she interrupted his thoughts. "You know as well as I do that she wouldn't swat a fly, which means that she's too sweet to tell you the truth," she said pointendly. "She's never going to tell you that things between you two will never work out, because she knows that it would crush you to pieces." She straightened and arched her brow at him. "So stop being weird about it and just accept the situation."

Despite having no reason to listen to this scowling woman, Noah found himself silent, taking in Jules' words.

"Why do you want a girl who has affection for another man? The entire town knows that Hottie and Chloe are in love. Why don't you?"

Ouch. He'd heard enough of uptight bun's pep talk. If she'd meant to shred Noah to pieces and crush his ego, she'd succeeded in that area.

Without another word, Noah turned and saw himself through the door. Even if Jules' words had seemed matter of fact, they weighed on him for the rest of the day as he finished the shelving unit at the shop and did his other projects.

In the silence of the night, Noah tossed and turned. *If you love her, you need to let her go*. Jules' words echoed in the back of his mind.

Why did Zach have to show up in town?

The sooner Noah finished Zach's house, the sooner the good doctor could sell it and leave town, and go off to another country or wherever. Guilt washed over Noah for even thinking like that.

He'd worked at Zach's house a few days ago when one of Noah's clients cancelled a project, and tomorrow he would work with him to fix the building for Chloe's fashion show.

The man was good looking, funny, and everybody fell in love with him the instant he spoke with them. On top of all that, he was good at what he did. The way Zach had taken charge when Garth fell off the horse, his genuine concern for the old man, and his determination to do everything in his power to assess each bone before they'd taken the patient to the hospital, had blown Noah away.

Of course he hadn't admitted it to Zach, but he was good. He had also done a procedure on Chloe's dad's back, and George hadn't complained about back issues ever since. The only pain came with his therapy sessions, but he was now a happy man.

Thinking about all of Zach's good qualities didn't help Noah get much sleep. Exhausted, he gulped almost three cups of dark roast the next morning before heading over to the Eron property.

The building, which had been the first home of the Eron family, was one rectangular room,with hardwood floors that needed to be polished. An addition had been added years ago so it could serve as a church, and later as a community room for events in town.

He worked alongside his men as they sawed and hammered wood into squares and rectangles to build a stage for Chloe's fashion show. Near the back of the building, Chloe stood in a circle with Zach and the stage designer. As much as Noah wanted to know what Chloe was laughing about, the pounding of hammers drowned out the group's voices, and Noah couldn't hear anything.

Earlier, the stage designer had walked through the instructions with Noah on what the stage should look like. From what Noah had gathered, it seemed the models were going to practice on how to walk on the stage a few days before the actual show.

He stared again where his eyes shouldn't. Chloe, taking notes on her iPad, chuckled again. Actually, all three of them were laughing – Zach, Chloe and the pony-tailed man. Her head leaned back, and Zach casually draped his arm over her shoulder. That's when Noah almost hammered his thumb, missing it by a millimeter.

Even though he had known Chloe for years, Noah didn't feel comfortable doing anything besides holding her hand, certainly not draping an arm over her shoulder. Zach, on the other hand, had only known Chloe for less than four months, yet he seemed to know her better, as if they belonged to each other.

The way Zach was taking this event so seriously was an indication of how much he loved Chloe. He'd hired the stage manager, who was his old friend, according to what Chloe had told Noah.

Zach and his friend exited the building, and Chloe strode towards the stage, stunning in her red polka dot maxi-dress.

Noah set the hammer down and dusted his hands off on his thick jeans before he left his men to meet Chloe.

"How did work go at Jim and Patty's house?" she asked.

He smiled, remembering the comical old man whom he'd gone to help install the bathroom sink. "Jim's jokes were tolerable, until Patty decided to join us, and smoked right next to me the entire time."

Chloe laughed, a smile he would miss when he couldn't get her to go on a date with him. "You should have reminded her of the dangers of smoking."

Chloe always had a way with people, and could get anybody to do whatever she requested. "If she doesn't listen to you, I'm not sure she would listen to anybody else."

"Thank you for always being willing to help," she said. "And thank you for doing this." She gestured her head around the house.

Noah scratched his head. "Zach did all this."

"I know you had a lot to do with it too."

"He's paying me...he insisted."

Her smile vanished, and she looked almost pained. "Can you please walk me back to the car?"

Oh...oh, he liked walking with her, but he suddenly felt unsettled. "Sure."

"I want you to know that no matter what, you will always be special to me," she said as they strode towards her car which was parked several yards away. "You're a good man, Noah...a good friend."

A friend? Thank goodness that she brought that brutal reminder to light. For a while he'd forgotten his place and assumed that they'd progressed to something more than friendship. Was this a goodbye? *Oh God, please not today!* He chuckled nervously and shoved his shaky hands into his pockets. "Should I be worried?"

As much as he'd known this day was coming, he didn't want to hear the parting words, not now while he needed to get her project done.

"You don't have to worry about anything, Noah. The entire town loves you."

Not exactly the answer he wanted to hear, but he finally let out the breath he had no idea he'd been holding.

After saying goodbye to Chloe, he carefully carried the new door to the door frame so he could install it while his men finished the stage.

"How can I help?"

Noah spun his head and looked at Zach, whose wavy hair looked more appropriate for a magazine cover than being a doctor, and definitely not for working on the door.

"I would make you work, if you weren't paying me."

"You said the project will get done sooner if you have as many people working as possible."

Noah turned his attention to the door and pushed it into place, trying to ignore Zach's scrutiny. He then stretched out his hand, struggling to reach for a jar of nails he'd left on the workbench.

Zach grabbed the glass jar and handed it to him. "I want to…I don't want Chloe to stress about the venue's progress."

Noah didn't want to work alongside Zach, not the man who was about to take Chloe away from him. Yet, Zach wasn't a show off, he just wanted to do the right thing. There were several reasons to like the guy, but he didn't want to like him, which made his chest hurt all the more.

"I could go work with your men instead." Zach's suggestion pulled him from his thoughts.

Seeing his determination, Noah was left with no option but to accept Zach's help. "Hold this." He traded the jar for the door, then he pulled a hinge from his pockets. Grabbing an electric screwdriver from the workbench, he powered the screws into place.

"I still can't believe that you made this door from scratch," Zach said, running his free hand over the finish.

Noah responded plainly, "Somebody's gotta do it."

Perhaps Zach got the memo in his tone, because he remained silent as they worked until Noah drilled the final hinge into place.

Needing to make amends for his flat tone, Noah offered, "Chloe tells me that you became a doctor... by inspiration from acting?" He picked up a loose nail and tossed it in the jar.

"Yes," was all Zach said.

"Did she tell you that I almost went into acting?"

Zach was silent for a moment as he brushed his hands together, ridding himself of sawdust. "No, she hasn't yet."

"I guess Chloe doesn't tell you a lot about me, does she?"

Zach gave Noah a sideways glance before he spoke. "She says that you're the most talented builder she's ever met."

Was that all she liked about him? He clamped and tightened the lid on the jar. "You need to stop leading Chloe on, since you're leaving."

That was totally uncalled for–he was pathetic, as Zach would say. Did he think that Zach was his son? Zach stared at him blankly, as if to say, *Seriously, dude?*

Trying to redeem himself, Noah came up with what he hoped was a better statement. "What are your intentions with Chloe?"

Zach chuckled, not that Noah could blame him. "Did she tell you to ask me those questions?"

"Of course she didn't."

"Then I'm afraid I will not be able to give you the answers you need."

Zach was right. Like a fool driven to desperation, he asked another question, "Do you love her?"

"Yes." Zach stared at him, his unwavering response making Noah's heart pound with fear. "I didn't expect to have a therapy session, but while we're at it, I might as well admit that I like her, but goodness, you're her family's hero. You're all she raves about whenever someone has a faucet that needs fixing or a home improvement project. So I can't be confident in saying that she's fully into me. Whether I force myself into her life or not, at some point, she'll have to make a choice between a man who never settles in one place, and the one who has a future in the town she loves." His voice lowered. "The guy who's always there for her and her family." Looking defeated, Zach raked a hand through his hair and strode off to the open field.

Wasn't it crystal clear that Chloe already belonged with Zach? Yet the man obviously still had doubts. Surely she wouldn't choose Noah over Zach? But since Zach was leaving, maybe Noah hadn't lost Chloe just yet. Perhaps Chloe would love him once Zach wasn't around to distract her.

Is that what he wanted to be? Her rebound guy? He wasn't sure what he wanted, except that he wanted Chloe in any form. Partial or whatever, he was not giving up just yet.

CHAPTER 14

The big day was finally here. A spacious canvas tent stood just outside the freshly renovated building. Chloe had rented it for the designers to store their goods in, and for the hairdressers and make-up artists to set up stations to tend to the models. Zach's sister Addie had brought her hair designer along, and Chloe had hired two local hair stylists.

Chloe stood behind a teal backdrop curtain that separated the backstage area from the room filled with over five hundred people waiting to see her fashions. Most of the audience had been shuttled in from town, but there were also several cars parked in the meadow.

Onstage, Zach gave the introductions, saying something that made the audience laugh. He spoke with such ease, while Chloe's own stomach trembled with nervousness, since she had no idea how to address a large crowd.

Zach had taken over the MC job after the original announcer came down with the flu. His place as a model had been passed onto a friend of his from Hollywood, who had originally bought a ticket to attend the fashion show.

"Tonight, Love's Boutique celebrates its new designs," Zach continued when the crowd's laughter had died down. "Button Theme Designs." After light applause from the audience, he said, "I will now introduce the designer. Without her, this event wouldn't be happening. Please join me in welcoming...Chloe Love!"

Chloe's heart thumped when Zach called her name. *Relax,* she reminded herself, taking a deep breath before emerging from behind the curtain onto the platform to face the packed room. She recognized many familiar faces of Eron's residents, but there were several new faces, too. The people wore styles ranging from business casual to cocktail outfits.

Zach handed her the microphone and whispered in her ear, "It's gonna be okay."

She somehow felt a few nerves settle after his reassuring words.

People clapped, and her eyes followed Zach as he joined his mom, Monique. Chloe had met Monique, a blue-eyed and fashionable Australian native, last night at Zach's house. She had told Chloe and Zach how she and his dad had fallen in love and stayed with each other for a year before he got deployed to Germany for three years. Unfortunately, she'd moved on by the time he returned.

When Chloe returned her gaze to the audience, all eyes were fixed on her. On the front row, she recognized one of the critics from New York. Her blood rushed with so much heat, she almost closed her eyes just so she could keep herself upright. Were her fashions worthy of this audience?

Just then she remembered how Zach had coached her over the last few days when she'd told him how nervous she was–to not doubt her fashions, that some would love it and some would hate it. As for speaking, he'd suggested she find a focal point and stick to it, or stare over people's heads.

Chloe cleared her throat before she spoke. "Thank you so much for being here, and for your generous support in buying the tickets. All the money raised from this event will help fund the building of the assisted living center for seniors in our community."

People clapped, and she waited until the applause subsided before continuing. "Without the help of so many people, this event wouldn't have been possible. She recognized Jeanie, Jules, Noah and Zach. Her head gaze from the last head in the corner and her eyes found Zach's, who gave her a thumbs up, an encouragement that she was doing great.

When she was done, Zach came back onstage. The buttons on his dark blazer brushed her arm when he bent close to her ear to whisper more praise about how great she'd done.

He took the microphone and announced, "Now the moment you've all been waiting for…"

The crowd's enthusiastic applause was silenced when the music started, and the female models emerged onto the catwalk, showcasing button detailed summer dresses as they sauntered down the white runway.

Most of the models were Chloe's friends, and then Zach's sister Addie, who had become a new friend. She'd even called two of her friends from Boston, models from the boutique where she'd worked before moving back to Eron.

Brent had agreed to model a suit and a fall sweater, since Hank was in jail, but then Zach had gone out of his way to recruit Addie's boyfriend as a model, since he was about the same height as Hank.

The show lasted for about fifteen minutes. Afterward, Chloe was thrilled to be approached by a couple of people in the fashion industry, who said they would be in touch with her.

Soon the lights strung outside the tent and the building were brightening the darkening sky. Most of the people climbed on the bus that would shuttle them back into town. Another bus would arrive soon to take some of Zach's friends to the airport.

Zach waved Chloe over so he could introduce them while they waited.

She spoke to Rahul, Zach's friend he'd introduced to Chloe last night. She asked more about his family in India.

"Zach has met my family," Rahul said. "He thought they were tolerable enough for him to want to come back and visit."

Chloe assumed the olive skinned man had a loving family, if they were anything like their son.

The conversation shifted to missionary work, and Rahul expressed his excitement about the New Zealand trip with Zach, and the jobs they both had lined up in the Netherlands afterwards.

Chloe had to cut their conversation short when her family approached to say good night to her. Jeanie left with George and Cynthia, and Chloe gave Noah a hug to thank him for his help.

"I'll go ahead and return the generator," Noah said, hugging her a bit longer than necessary, until Chloe had to wiggle out of the embrace.

Chloe had rented the generator as a backup should they lose power. "I can take it back tomorrow in case you need to get home."

"One less thing to store overnight," Noah said and waved at her before he left.

With the building now emptied of people, Chloe took a deep breath as she stashed the center pieces in a box. Only one table was left standing in the room, which had belonged to Zach's grandparents.

Muffled footsteps caused her to turn, and she saw Zach sauntering toward her. His suit jacket was gone, and the top button undone on his white shirt, which glistened a shimmery gold in the bright lights. *He's devastatingly handsome!*

"I'll clean that tomorrow," he said, taking the candle holder from her hand to set it on the table. He then took her hand in his. Her heart rate shot up at the hum of awareness that rippled between them, and she whispered his name.

Chloe's high heels put her at almost level height with him, and she swallowed. She told herself she needed to create distance between them, only to find that she didn't want to. "Thank you so much for everything," she whispered instead.

His breath was warm on her face. "I couldn't have done it without Noah."

It was true that Noah had done most of the manual work, but Zach had paid for it, not letting Chloe or Noah pay for anything that involved fixing the house. Zach had also made extra calls to gather media production personnel, and all the friends that he'd conjured up to give Chloe some ideas how to run a successful fashion show.

'Thank you' didn't even come close to being enough.

When Zach walked into the event house to look for Chloe, his intentions were to let her know that he wouldn't hold anything against her if she wanted to move on with Noah. The way Noah had lingered in Chloe's embrace when she was saying goodbye had been a reminder to Zach that he wasn't the only one who found Chloe attractive, and he also wasn't the only one who wanted her to be his forever.

The off-the-shoulder yellow dress looked stunning on her, and brought out a burnished glow on her skin. Zach had yet to see a color that she didn't look beautiful in.

The two times he'd worked beside Noah had helped Zach realize that he was a decent man. Even though he acted standoffish, Zach knew it was all because of Noah's fear of losing Chloe.

Setting his selfish reasons aside was the reason he was here–to let Chloe go. Well, not exactly, because he couldn't bear to do that, but to at least give her the chance to make her own decision.

"Why are you not visiting with your family?" Chloe's voice cut into his thoughts.

He blinked. "I have something for you." He dropped her hand and patted his dark dress pants before he shoved a hand in his pocket. He pulled out a black velvet pouch. "Thought I would give it to you on my last day in town, but I noticed that you didn't wear a necklace tonight." It could have waited until tomorrow, but he needed an excuse to talk to her.

Her eyes sparkled under the lights when she recognized the lariat-sterling silver necklace as he pulled it from the pouch and dangled it in front of her. "I had you in mind when I bought this, the first day I came to your shop."

Her lips parted. "I didn't think...how did I not keep track of the necklaces you sent your mom?"

He'd set it aside for her in the bag with the clothes he'd bought from her shop. "I have my ways."

He shoved the velvet pouch back in his pocket and moved behind her. "Let me help you get this on." Her hair brushed his fingers when he slid the necklace over her head. "When you tried this on that day, I knew that it belonged to you," he whispered in her ear. His shaky hands managed to snap the clasp closed, and they brushed against her flesh, sending a reaction through his arm that rippled through his body like a live wire. She smelled like flowers, a fresh scent that caused Zach's hands to linger on her neck a little longer than needed.

She tilted her head to the side. "I wish I had a mirror to see how it looks on me."

The breakout of goosebumps on her bare shoulder let Zach know that he wasn't the only one feeling this. No doubt she felt a reaction as much as he did. He spun her around. "Let me be your mirror."

He then curled his fingers around the sparkling diamonds that encircled the emerald pendant. His fingers brushed her chest and she gasped.

"You look...beautiful." He dropped his hand to his side and peered into her soft eyes. "You're perfect, and the necklace suits you." He reached out to touch the two brown buttons on her other shoulder. He had no idea if she'd designed the dress as a display for her event or if it was hers to keep. "This dress, can you not sell it?"

She bobbed a nod. Her breathing quickened, and her eyes dropped to his mouth. Zach had the same idea, although he didn't intend on staring at her lips, because he'd done that several times and dreamed about the moment he would place his lips on hers. He hoped his button up shirt hid his racing pulse.

He closed the gap between them and cupped her face. He looked down at her, at her soft skin so perfect and right. *What is wrong with you, Zach?* He wished he knew, because he felt out of control when it came to Chloe.

When she breathed his name, what he saw in her eyes made his heart stagger. Zach forgot all the reasons why Noah was the perfect guy for her. Bending slightly, he claimed her mouth greedily. His heart pounded, and his pulse hammered out of control. *Slow down.*

He ignored the small voice as he devoured her fiercely. He liked the feel of her fingers in his hair. Thankfully Chloe was just as responsive, and drowning in his arms.

Good grief, just slow down! Zach reluctantly tore his lips from hers and waited another moment, their lips a whisper apart, giving Chloe the chance to push him away, praying that she wouldn't.

Breathless, Chloe fluttered her eyes open.

"I'm sorry I couldn't resist…"

She reached up and pulled him back down to her, and the rest of his words were lost against her mouth. He kissed her gently and carefully this time, savoring the warmth of her lips. Chloe clutched the collar of his shirt, clinging onto it like her life depended on it. Zach wrapped his arm around her back to keep her from falling. She tasted so good, like sweet summer fruit, even better than he'd imagined, better than anything he'd ever experienced before.

She suddenly pulled away, trembling as she created distance between them, as if snapping out of it. Her hand flew to her chest, followed by a frown. She looked frazzled.

If Zach had not felt the passion from her kisses, he would be hurt by her reaction right now, but he couldn't when all he wanted to do was sweep her up in his arms and kiss her all over again.

"I...I need to tell Noah that..." she breathed. "I need to talk to him first." Her eyes searched his face, a mixture of longing and confusion in them as she stared at his lips, as if wanting a repeat of what they'd just shared, yet struggling.

Of course she liked Noah, or loved him. "Its okay," Zach said, wanting to make her decision easier.

"I'm going to leave now." She pointed towards the door, although not moving. "I...I will leave."

Confused, Zach nodded slowly. "Night."

She looked a little shaky before she turned to leave, and that's when Zach's mind awoke. He needed to say something, to pour out his heart, even if things didn't make sense.

"Chloe, wait!" he called after her, and she turned and froze.

Zach's body burned with fear. His life and choices stood in the balance. This was different, Chloe was different. He would move on if she decided to give Noah a chance, but Zach trembled at the possibility of losing her.

He took a step back–a safe distance was much needed, because he might be too nervous and end up doing something foolish, like kissing her again. She'd acted like she didn't want him to, yet her face showed otherwise.

Setting his selfish desires aside, Zach cleared his throat before his dreaded speech. "I want you to know that I love you. I'm in love with you, Chloe, and that's the only reason I want to leave this decision up to you, to give you the chance to make a choice."

Forcing the words, he continued, "I want you to have the chance to make a choice between me and Noah. I know that I've been hovering over you and haven't given you time to think through things."

She let out a shuddering breath and pressed her hands to her cheeks.

"Gosh, Chloe, I don't even know where I'll be next month, now that the doctor will return to work in two weeks. I don't know what my future looks like, and I don't have a plan like Noah does. The one thing I know is that I want you in my crazy life. I want to figure this out with you, to figure it out together."

She was silent, taking in all his words.

"That's why I want you to think through this. I'm leaving… I have no choice, since I made a commitment to return to New Zealand for six months." He wanted to ask her to go with him, but that would be too much to ask of her when she had a family to take care of. No doubt she was going to be contacted by fashion houses after tonight's fashion show.

"I don't want to rush you into making a decision before you're ready. I know that Noah has everything you need, and he means a lot to your family, and I don't want to take that away from you. I will always love you, no matter what choice you make. You're the best thing that ever happened to me."

She rubbed a hand over her eyes. Was she crying? He hated to cause any tears for her.

"Oh, Zach." She spoke between gasped breaths before she strode to Zach and wrapped her arms around him. He breathed in the soft fragrance of her conditioner, savored her soft curls rubbing against his jaw. He kissed the top of her hair and fought the urge to stare into her eyes. He wanted to hold her like this forever and never have to let her go.

Even though she didn't say the words *I love you*, for now he was content in her warm embrace, knowing deep down that she had room in her heart for him. He just wasn't sure if that room was enough to trample the mountain in their path. "Good night, Chloe."

And just like that, she was gone, and Zach knew he would be up for the rest of the night, staring at the intricate ceiling but seeing only her.

CHAPTER 15

"**I** love you, too, Zach, and always will!" Chloe finally uttered the words out loud to herself as she turned down the unlit winding road that led to her house. Words she'd held back from telling Zach. Especially since her tongue had gone numb from that knee weakening kiss they'd shared. And more so, she needed to speak to Noah first.

What was she thinking falling for Zach? The man was leaving. Leaving. Leaving!

Did you hear him say that he was leaving?

Yes.

Then why is he consuming your mind?

She knew the answer to that–because she loved him more than she'd ever loved or felt for someone before. She loved her mom and step dad, and she loved her grandma more than anything, but loving Zach consumed her mind and filled all her senses. It was the kind of love that would be hard to explain to anybody.

That night, when Chloe got home, she threw herself onto the hardwood floor, not caring that it was cold—she had bigger issues to worry about than the cold from the floor seeping through her body. Her mind wouldn't focus on anything, couldn't think of anything or anybody but Zach. Even though she wanted to avoid them, the raging emotions consumed her mind.

How was she going to break it to Noah? She had attempted that when he'd worked at the house on Zach's property, but she'd held back the moment Noah asked if he should be worried. Like the coward she was, she had put off ending whatever they had going.

She tried to force Zach out of her mind. Perhaps doing that would shed some light on her dilemma.

Noah. He was steady in town, he had plans for their future, and had built a house already. He helped her family a lot. Oh, there was an even bigger reminder to not entertain her own desires when there was her family to consider.

'*I love you...you're the best thing that ever happened to me.*' Zach's words echoed in the back of her mind.

Zach or Noah? She banged her forehead on the floor, in search for an answer. *Zach!* Came the small voice. She groaned, dreading that day when she had to talk to Noah.

"Oh, God, why does this have to be hard? Why should I have to be the one to break up with Noah? Can't he break up with me instead? That would be so much easier!" she spoke out loud.

Her answer came when the doorbell rang. She dragged herself up from the floor and plodded to the front door. Peeking through the peephole, she gasped at the sight of the familiar silhouette backlit by the security lights.

She yanked the door open. "Noah, what are you…"

"Listen, Chloe!" he panted, his arms hanging loosely at his sides, and his slacks and blue striped, button up shirt rumpled as if he'd been running. "I love you, and you know that I do."

He threw his hands up in exasperation. "Good grief, I don't even have to tell you this. It's like I'm carrying a neon sign everywhere I go. Without you, my future is a mess. Every time I close my eyes, I see you. Everytime I think of success, you're right there beside me. Wait...wait." He took a deep breath. "Chloe, what I'm trying to say is that you complete me, you make me want to be a better man. When I started building the house, I had you in mind. I picture our kids running around…"

He rambled on with an endless list, but Chloe tuned his voice out. She couldn't bear to listen to all the plans he'd made for them to be together.

She buried her face in her hands, trying to force herself to tell Noah that things would never work between them, that her heart had been captured by Zach, but the words wouldn't come out. Despite her best efforts, her silent tears turned into loud, hiccupping sobs.

He reached out and placed a hand on her shoulder. "Chloe, what's wrong? Are you okay?"

Unable to speak through her tears, Chloe just shook her head.

"What can I do to help?" Noah asked, and his kindness set off a fresh round of sobs. "Tell me what's wrong so I can help."

She reached for the cascading ruffle on her dress and swiped her eyes, then forced out the words, "Please, Noah, I... need to be alone, okay?"

Noah took his hand off her and stepped back, then let out a slow breath. "Okay, I'll go, but I will see you...soon."

She couldn't even watch him leave, since her face was covered by her fingers, and she'd lost her voice to utter another word. When the door closed quietly behind him, Chloe leaned against it and slid to the floor, overwhelmed by guilt. How could she hurt him?

The rest of the night was rough–she couldn't sleep, couldn't make a decision. Tired of tossing and turning, she drove to her grandma's house, needing to talk to her. Jeanie was the only person she'd always felt was wise enough whenever she needed counsel. And Jeanie had always made herself available for Chloe to talk to her anytime she needed. Night or day, she had always been there.

Only the chirping of crickets split the silence of the night as she got out of her car. Since she still had a key to the house, Chloe let herself in. The house was quiet, the lights turned off. Chloe stood outside Jeanie's room and let out a shuddering breath.

She closed her eyes for a moment as memories from her past washed over her. Her, around nine years old, at a different house but standing in the same place–waiting outside her grandma's door, crying and looking for answers when mean girls had made fun of her mom, for being a stray because of the fact that Chloe didn't even have a dad.

"Never let anyone's mean remark create a dent in your spirit," Jeanie had said. "All that matters is what God thinks of you." She then reminded Chloe of the same words she'd always told her. "You're important and special. Never doubt that you are loved. I always doubted my choices and how I raised Cynthia, but God gave me another chance to be a parent, and seeing how wonderfully you've turned out has showed me know that I'm not as bad a parent after all." She'd said those words on more than one occasion.

Chloe gave a soft knock before letting herself into Grandma's room, the same way she'd always done when she needed to talk or cry. She tiptoed in and heard Grams jump out of her covers in the darkened room.

"Is that you, Sunshine?"

"Yes, Grandma," she whispered.

"Come lay down next to me." Jeanie climbed back in bed and made room for Chloe to join her.

Chloe slid under the covers and was immediately comforted when Jeanie's familiar lavender scent engulfed her. She shuddered, and Grandma wrapped an arm around her.

"Oh, my dear child. What's wrong, Sunshine?"

Chloe described how she felt about the two men in her life, and her struggle to make the right choice. "How will that leave things for you guys if you can't get Noah's help anymore?"

Grams was silent for a while as she brushed loose strands of hair from Chloe's face. "It's not fair to you or Noah if you don't tell him the truth. Marrying him because of what he does for our family would be even worse," she finally said. "This is your life, Sunshine, not ours. I made a choice to not remarry once your grandpa died. Your ma made her own choices too, and it's now your turn to decide." Her hands continued to gently stroke Chloe's hair. "Zach helped take care of George, and pretty soon, he will be in good shape to do the work himself. Someday, your parents and I will die or be in the nursing home that you're so generously providing. I don't think we will be required to shovel snow or mow the lawn there."

Chloe had no idea what to say to that, except that her grandma's words were always insightful.

"You have to tell Noah, no matter what," Jeanie insisted.

"But Zach is leaving."

"Whether he's leaving or not, your heart doesn't belong to Noah. I see how relaxed and happy you are when Zach is around. You remind me of the time when I had just fallen in love with your grandpa." She chuckled as if visiting a memory of her own. "I'm sure that Zach's heart belongs to you, too. God will take care of Noah, and He will take care of you and Zach. Leave the burdens to God. I know that you take care of everybody else and tend to forget to take care of yourself."

Jeanie then quoted the Bible verse that she always told her whenever she had a struggle or a problem. "Cast your burdens on Jesus, for He cares for you." She continued gently stroking Chloe's hair and reminded her of all the reasons she wasn't responsible for anybody else's burdens.

Chloe's eyes felt heavy and she finally gave in to the pull of sleep.

It was two days since Chloe's fashion show, and her meltdown over her dilemma with the two men in her life. When she showed up after her morning meeting with the fundraiser committee for the nursing home, two bouquets awaited her on the counter.

She didn't need a note to know that the red roses came from Noah and the ranunculus from Zach. She had taken a couple of days off from texting either Noah or Zach, just so she could clear her mind and pray. It was a relief that neither of them had bothered to text or call her.

Jules smiled at her, a real smile this time.

"What did I do to deserve your generous smile today?" Chloe asked, flopping onto the couch.

Jules chuckled. "You're in trouble, I can confidently say." She glanced over her shoulder to the refrigerator in the corner, then said, "Hottie brought you a slice of cheesecake, too. I put it in the refrigerator."

Chloe smiled. "Cheesecake, huh?"

Jules brought her laptop and joined her on the couch. "He told me to tell you that they only had one slice left at the cake shop, and as badly as he wanted it, he decided to let you have it."

The fact that Jules was relaying all this information was alarming. She rarely gave people the chance to finish what they had to say. "How did Zach get you to be the messenger?"

She shrugged. "I told him that I don't play mail lady, but he kept talking and said that he trusted me to tell you, since I'm closer to you than anybody."

"I hope you didn't scare him off."

She rolled her eyes. "Like he's one to scare off!" She then shifted her eyes back to the computer. "Okay, enough with your love triangle. We have some exciting emails here."

Chloe scooted next to Jules as she scrolled through the inbox. She suddenly remembered the package she'd received in the mail yesterday. "By the way, thank you for the buttons."

Jules tore her gaze from the computer and stared at her. "It's not the best housewarming present, but since you have a thing for buttons, I figured…" She shrugged.

Warmed by her thoughtful gesture, Chloe gave Jules a side hug. "I love them. With that big box, it will be several years before I shop for buttons."

"That was my point." Jules turned back to the computer and read an email out loud from a fashion house in L.A . "Your button theme designs would be perfect for our fall line up. Please contact us as soon as possible so we can discuss featuring your designs."

Chloe's heart leaped in excitement, or was it fear? She exhaled.

"You're in for more psychological torture if you ask me. We'll need to grow our team of employees if you accept this offer," Jules warned, then she read another email from a critic in New York: "Would love for you to come to my Black and White party next week. I will transport you."

Chloe had to scratch her head as Jules read more emails. She hadn't expected major orders when she did the show. She had only wanted to raise money for the senior center, which thankfully, they had. Donations from the people who attended the show, along with ticket sales, had raised a little over five million dollars.

After they'd finished reading the messages and going over the figures, Chloe mulled over what Jules had said. June normally brought more tourists into the boutique, but since the show, the place had been bustling. Chloe assumed the day's extra busy-ness was due to the fashion show's media exposure.

Right now, she was dealing with a new customer who wanted a custom wedding dress designed. Chloe didn't usually design wedding dresses, but it was hard to say no once the woman pulled out her phone to show her one of Chloe's cocktail dresses on Love's website. The customer wanted her wedding dress to look similar, and Chloe was able to sketch a rough draft of the design.

Carl, the teenager who normally helped out in the summertime, brought their lunch just as Chloe finished talking to the woman. Sofia joined them from her office upstairs. Thankfully, Jules and Sofia had reconciled after their argument last time, and Jules was looking forward to being a bridesmaid at her cousin's wedding.

While the three girls ate lunch, Jules told them about her step dad's upcoming harp performance at church on Sunday. "He wants me to come and watch him play." She wrinkled her nose.

Chloe swallowed a bite of cucumber-avocado salad, and Sofia dug her fork back into her Caesar salad. "Are you going to come?"

"That depends on the dress code." Jules stared at Chloe, who couldn't contain her smile. "I don't want to be dressed in a gown of some sort." She then arched a brow. "And if everybody at your church smiles at me like that, I will leave right away." She finally bit into her avocado sandwich.

"Nobody is going to smile, Jules," Chloe lied–there would be several happy faces ready to greet and embrace Jules at the door when she walked into the church. "Except for me, of course."

Chloe and Sofia had stopped inviting Jules to church after several weeks of her declining their invitations. Whether she made it to church or not, the fact that she was entertaining the idea was reason enough to celebrate.

While Sofia talked about her last minute wedding plans, Chloe's mind wandered to the dreaded dinner that Noah had invited her to tonight.

"Chloe?"

She shook her head to snap herself out of her stupor. "Yes...yes I'm looking forward to that, too?"

Sofia smiled at Chloe's absent minded response. She set her empty plate aside and peered at Chloe. "What's going on? You're totally not yourself."

"The break-up dinner she has tonight with Noah." Jules bit into her sandwich again.

"Oh, boy." Sofia gritted her teeth and toned her voice to a whisper. "Noah's sister told Keisha's friend that he's going to propose tonight."

Chloe's stomach churned. No wonder he'd suggested they meet at the high-end restaurant for dinner. She stared at her half-eaten salad and picked up the fork, then moved it around the green meal, suddenly not hungry. "What am I going to do?"

"Noah is established in town," Sofia said, tapping her manicured fingernails on the table. "Zach is leaving soon, but..."

"You already know what to do," Jules interjected. "Otherwise you wouldn't be struggling. The truth is bitter, but it's your ticket to freedom."

Chloe knew Jules was right. '...The truth will set you free.' The verse she'd read before, not sure from what book of the Bible, echoed in the back of her mind. She had a more godly perspective on things than Jules, yet she wished she had a slight bit of Jules' bluntness. She shoved the salad to the side. "Okay, I guess today is that day." She sighed.

"You're really making such a big deal about this." Jules dabbed a napkin to her lips and tossed it across the empty plate. "You have the attention of two handsome men, and you think that's a reason to be mourning?"

"You don't understand."

Jules' face turned serious. She didn't seem upset, but was just being honest like she always was. "You're right, I don't understand. I fell for a guy–an ex-convict for that matter–just because I liked his dragon tattoo." She shook her head and continued. "You have Sweet Pea, who doesn't have a dark side, then there's Hottie, who looks like he's just stepped off a magazine cover. You both sacrifice cheesecakes for each other."

Sofia and Chloe exchanged glances before turning back to Jules. The corners of her lips curved, was she smiling? Chloe frowned, pondering why Jules would be smiling after giving a personal pep talk.

"A dragon tattoo," Jules said softly. "What kind of person falls in love with someone because they like their tattoos?" She then burst out in laughter.

Chloe glanced at Sofia and they both joined in the chorus of laughter.

It felt good to laugh, or more importantly, to see Jules laughing. It didn't matter what they were laughing about, but

Chloe had forgotten that Jules could be hilarious when she decided to.

When Chloe arrived at the restaurant Noah had chosen, he smiled at her, a warm and hopeful smile that only increased her feelings of dread for what she was about to do to him.

The French Cuisine was upscale and pricey, so when the waiter seated them, Chloe asked for only a Sprite, and a separate check. At Noah's questioning look, she explained that she wasn't hungry.

"I kissed Zach," were the first words out of her mouth once the waiter left.

He stared at the chandelier above Chloe's head, as if letting her words sink in. A moment passed before he spoke. "That was a mistake," he said, searching her eyes. "I know Zach forced his way into your life...into our lives."

Chloe stared at him, knowing that Zach hadn't forced his way into her heart.

After a moment, Noah asked, "When did this happen?"

"After the show."

He clenched his jaw and closed his eyes for a second. After taking a deep breath to calm himself, Noah opened his eyes. "He's leaving."

"I know."

"I forgive you. Just tell me that you don't love him."

She let out a slow breath and buried her face in both hands. Her silence should have been answer enough, yet he still repeated the statement. "Tell me, Chloe, that you are not in love with Zach."

Chloe couldn't look a him, afraid to meet disappointment in his face. "Noah... I can't... I can't say that."

"Forget about Zach. He's leaving in less than two months, maybe even sooner, and we'll get our lives back. I want you to give us a chance." His voice was tinged with desperation.

Her heart torn to pieces, she pulled herself together enough to choke out the words, "I...I like you, Noah. You're a very good man." She shook her head. "But I'm in love with Zach, and I can't keep on misleading you."

Noah stared down at the table for so long Chloe wondered if he was all right. She wanted to take his hand, to comfort him, but that would send a mixed message, and so she waited.

He finally raised his head when the waiter deposited his food, but he didn't look at Chloe. Staring off to one side like he was watching his dreams fade away, he spoke in a soft, steady voice, almost as if to himself. "I always knew that you were out of my league. I guess I should have known better. I should've left you alone."

He tossed some money on the table for his food, stood up, and slowly walked out of the restaurant without looking back.

The next morning, Chloe emerged from the shower, wishing she felt more refreshed than she'd been before she'd stepped into the bathroom. She pulled on her leggings and threw on a sweater before texting Jules that she would be late for work today. She needed to write handwritten thank you's to all the people who had contributed to the show.

At least that was the excuse she gave Jules. The truth was, she needed some time to herself after last night. It had been a long night of heartache and shedding tears for what she had done to Noah, and she had barely managed to pull herself together this morning.

She burst into tears all over again when she remembered Noah's saddened face and his parting words.

Oh dear God, what have I done? A fresh wave of grief engulfed her, and she threw herself back onto the bed, burying her head underneath her pillow

CHAPTER 16

'Noah is proposing tonight.' Those were the words Zach had heard last night from two nurses whispering by the vending machine at the hospital. The words felt like a live wire coursing through his body while he'd finalized his shift.

Having not heard from Chloe for the last three days since they'd kissed, Zach was starting to panic that he'd lost her to Noah. Had she said yes to Noah's proposal? That, and the call he'd received from the realtor about a new offer for his house, had kept him tossing and turning throughout the night. He had less than ten days left at the hospital, since the doctor was now feeling better and would resume his duties soon.

After downing two cups of coffee, Zach stared at the clock on his phone and realized it was still only five. There were several things he could do with his time, like going to the gym, reading his Bible, or praying. He tried to do the latter, except his thoughts were too scattered.

"Forgive me, Lord!" he said, and pulled himself up to take his shower.

He pulled on his gray pants and a flannel shirt, then grabbed his black work bag, and sped down the stairs, closing the door behind him without locking it. Forgetting what he'd told Chloe about giving her time to make a choice, Zach felt an urgency to find out if he still had a chance with her, if her choices still included him.

The darkness of night was giving way to light as Zach drove down an unpaved dirt road with nothing but undeveloped land on both sides. The gentle lowing of cattle drew his attention to a small herd of black cows grazing in the open pasture.

Seven miles later, he made another turn. The early morning silence was broken by the revving of his car engine as he sped over the winding road to Chloe's house.

His heart pounded when he cut the engine in Chloe's driveway.

"Commit everything you do to the Lord. Trust Him and He will help you." The words he'd read last night from Psalm 37 replayed in his mind. He'd tried to cling to that verse last night when he attempted to read his Bible.

I can do this, Lord. I know that You've got this situation under control! He stepped out of his Land Rover, his steps becoming more uncertain the closer he got to the front door.

He let out an exhale and ran a hand through his hair as he debated whether to use the doorbell or knock. He raised his knuckles to the door and knocked softly, in case she was sleeping in this morning.

"A great offer. You could walk away a happy man." The realtor's words echoed in the back of his mind as he waited. The buyer was willing to pay way more than asking price, and wanted the entire property. That's what Zach had wanted in the first place, to get an offer for both the house and property so he could leave the small town. Why wasn't he happy now that his dream had come true?

He knew why–it had everything to do with the Black beauty he was about to leave behind to a man who was ready to step into Zach's place as soon as he left.

Things were coming together to speed his departure, yet he was now in no hurry to be anywhere but Eron–with Chloe.

He lifted his knuckles to knock again, but the door swung open and his hand froze in mid-air at his princess's downcast face.

"Chloe!" He dropped his hand to his side and stared down at her swollen eyes, then her outfit. Her cropped brown tights and off-the-shoulder green sweater told him she's already been awake. A yellow hair band was wrapped around her rumpled hair. Not exactly dressed for work. She could easily go to work just like that, but Chloe always dressed fashionably at her shop.

Unsure of what to say, he stepped forward and enveloped her in a hug. She tightened her arms around him. Had she accepted Noah's proposal and was now realizing she'd made a mistake?

"I broke... I..." Her words came in gasps, as if she was ready to explode into tears. "I..."

"Everything's gonna be okay. Let's go sit down." He closed the door with his foot while holding onto her, not wanting to let go. Was he the reason for her tears? His heart lurched at the possibility.

"Oh, Princess." He settled her on the sofa, then sat next to her, their feet resting on the colorful rug.

"I broke Noah's heart, Zach." She struggled to meet his eyes, and her lips quivered.

Zach had never seen her in this state. He held one of her warm hands in his, and relief surged through him when he saw no ring on her finger. *God forgive me for being selfish,* he spoke in his heart. Chloe's words now registered. She'd either declined Noah's proposal, or she had ended things between them.

Zach turned and cupped her chin so he could peer at her, then moved his fingers along her smooth jaw. "I'm sorry that you're hurting," he whispered. "It doesn't surprise me that you feel terrible about your conversation with Noah. You are you, Chloe–you love people, and you hate to see anybody get hurt."

Her eyes lost some of their anguish and she let out a silent sigh. He had no idea what else to say, yet he didn't want to ask about the details of her conversation with Noah, just in case she was struggling about whether to let Noah go.

He pulled her close and she rested her head on his shoulder. She slid her arm around his waist and they sat in silence for several minutes.

Torn between staying or leaving for work with her in this state, he asked, "Are you going to work today?"

She responded with a soft nod.

"Will it be okay if I stop by the shop during my lunch break?"

"I would love that."

He reluctantly released her and stood up.

She did the same. "Thanks for stopping by."

Thanks was just a simple word, but he felt relieved to know that he hadn't been intruding on her, and that she was glad he'd stopped by.

He stepped forward. "I'll see you soon." Cupping the back of her head, he pressed a kiss to her forehead. It was only logical he should move to the door and leave, but his legs didn't seem to get the message.

With his hand still behind her head, he took a moment to admire her face, especially her moist lips. Her eyes too soft when she stared at him intently, his heartbeat quickened and he shifted his gaze to her long curly hair that begged to be touched. He did just that, gently moving the loose strands of hair from her forehead and tucking them underneath the yellow headband. He was totally caught by surprise when Chloe stood on tiptoes and gripped his collar, pulling him to her and planting her soft lips on his.

It seemed out of character for her to make such a bold move, but he wasn't about to complain while he was enjoying the taste of her fruit scented lips. Her full lips were warm against his, and he let her have control for about two seconds before he deepened the kiss. Chloe gasped when his fingers threaded into her hair, which was soft as silk and smelled of vanilla.

"I...I love you, Zach," she spoke breathlessly when they caught a breath between the kisses.

Those words brought his lips back to hers again, carefully, soft and tender this time. He felt as if he would be doing the same thing with her everyday for the rest of his life. He then reminded himself to slow down so he could get to work, hoping to see Chloe in a few hours. He reluctantly pulled away from her, breathing in gasps, and then planted another kiss on her forehead.

"We need to be careful," he said, since his body was turned upside down.

"I know," Chloe said.

With a promise to see her in a few, he left for work. Going through his morning routine, he counted down the minutes until he would see her over his lunch break, which came before he knew it.

The rest of the week flew by, with Chloe spending every afternoon with him. One evening, they'd gone to Bingo night with the seniors and had dinner afterwards with one of Chloe's senior friends, most of whom were now Zach's friends, too. They had also signed up for three dancing classes in preparation for Sofia's wedding. Yesterday, they'd taken their first class.

Today dawned bright and sunny, and Chloe met Zach by the meadow on his property. They enjoyed a picnic on the freshly cut grass underneath a tree. Afterwards, they sat side by side on a dirt patched hill, Chloe's head leaning on his shoulder, Zach's arm around her waist, as they admired the colorful sunset. The bold brushstrokes of orange, with splashes of red woven in like a horizontal ribbon, made for a sight that was as refreshing and soothing as the woman next to him.

"What if God doesn't want you to be entangled in a relationship?" Chloe asked suddenly, breaking the silence.

The same question had honestly crossed his mind and had sent him to his knees, crying out to God that he could have both Chloe and still be able to do what he did. It had never occurred to him to pray for a spouse until he met Chloe. "I'm sure God can do something about it."

God could very well have different plans for Zach, plans that didn't include Chloe. His limbs started shaking at the prospect of not having Chloe in his life.

"What's going on in that busy mind of yours?" Even without meeting his gaze, she could probably feel his tension.

Not wanting to dwell on the distressing possibility, he chose to change the subject. "I see why my grandma liked watching sunsets."

Chloe moved her gaze from the sunset to him. "You do?"

"Yes, and I would like to make this a weekly..." The words failed when he remembered the dreadful decision he had to make. It was supposed to be a simple choice when he'd first stepped into town. Now things had gotten complicated. The buyer of his house was still waiting for his response. He didn't want to tell Chloe about the offer yet, not until he knew what he was going to do. He said instead, "So, my grandpa was ornery, huh?"

She chuckled and nodded slowly. "Just like you."

She'd told him all about his grandparents' life, at least most of the events and stories she knew, and all Zach needed to know. His roots were calling to him, and Eron was starting to feel like home.

"Oh, Zach," she spoke. "I'm going to miss you so much."

His chest tightened, holding back a lump that was forming in his throat. *Come with me.* He felt the urge to invite her, but it would be too much to ask from her. Would she even agree to it?

For the first time during his trips overseas, Zach dreaded his departure. "I'll miss you the most."

She tapped her head. "By the way, I auctioned my faith diamond on ebay, and it sold for six times more than I paid for it. I'm contributing $50,000 for your trip."

"You are not going to do anything of the sort." Zach kissed the tip of her ear and she giggled.

Serious again, she insisted, "I feel God has put it on my heart. You had plans to go back and work in LA to pay for your trip, but instead, you got caught up here in my town helping me and my people. I know the hospital barely pays you."

Once she put God in the picture, Zach decided not to argue.

Her gaze returned to the fading colors in the sky, and she continued. "I also spoke to the fundraising committee, and we agreed to take some of the money raised and add it to your trip, too." She peered at him. "Thanks to you, we raised over five million dollars in tickets and extra donations, and there are still more donations coming in."

She told him amount from her jewelry and from the committee, and Zach blinked in surprise at how God had provided. He still had some money in his account, but not enough for his lodging for six months. With that lump sum, Zach's problem if he chose not to sell the property would be solved, since he had hoped to apply some of the money from the sale to his trip.

The rest of the evening, they talked about the future, including his plan to return to Eron to check on her before he left for the Netherlands for two years.

By the time they left the meadow to head to Chloe's car, the sky was darkening, which meant it was probably eight or so. After kissing her goodnight, Zach set the picnic basket in the back of her car and shut the door.

He stared up at the sky, and the moon with random stars gleaming. Chloe's engine reved when she started the car and Zach was suddenly hit with a feeling of loneliness. He wasn't ready for her to leave, didn't want her to go. If he couldn't bear to be separated from her for a few hours, how was he going to survive six months without her? He stood by her window and rapped his knuckles gently against the glass.

She rolled down her window. "Did I forget something?"

He leaned forward and planted a kiss on her cheek, which somehow led to kissing her lips for what might have been a minute or two, but Zach wasn't counting. "Stay with me for a little bit longer."

She let out a shuddering breath, and the faint moonlight danced on her arched eyebrows.

"Let's sit on the deck and watch the stars," Zach suggested.

"I...I don't think it's a good idea." Her voice came out soft and weak. "I thought we had agreed to stay away from each other's houses."

Since they couldn't seem to keep their hands off each other, and with the passionate kisses they shared lately, they'd both agreed to not hang out at his house or her house, to avoid any intimate situations that would lead to something neither of them could resist.

He stepped back from her car and put up his hands. "I promise to keep two inches between us, and no kissing for the rest of the night," he said. "Except for the goodnight kiss when I walk you back to your car."

She was silent, as if considering his suggestion.

"I'll get your favorite quilt to keep you warm," he coaxed. They'd retrieved it from the mounds of boxes in the basement.

She cut the engine, then swung open the door. "Did you, by any chance, do sales before you became a doctor?"

Excitement coursed through Zach as he took her hand and traced slow circles on it with his thumb. "Not until recently. I thought I'd practice my sales pitch in case I end up working in your boutique."

True to his word, he refrained from touching Chloe while they gazed at the stars and talked about their future plans, such as her trip to the Black and White banquet in New York next week.

Several hours later, he kissed her goodnight as promised. "I love you, Chloe," he said and she said it back to him before she stepped into her car.

Zach fell asleep that night in a cocoon of contentment and indescribable joy. There were no words to describe his current state. He thought his heart might explode with happiness.

That feeling stayed with him for most of the next day, until she sent him a mid-morning text saying she was canceling their dance class for that evening, with no explanation.

When he texted her back, she never responded. He suffered through a dreadful afternoon until the end of the day, when he made it to her shop.

She was chatting and smiling with Jules when he entered her shop, but the moment she lifted her head and saw Zach, her smile vanished.

"Hi, Zach!" Jules greeted, which was alarming, since the woman had never initiated a greeting before. She then turned to leave. "I'll leave you two."

Something must have happened—why else would Jules offer to leave them alone? Chloe fiddled with her fingers, popping her knuckles furiously, a sure sign that she was upset.

"What's wrong, Princess?" He lowered himself to slide next to her on the sofa.

"Call me Chloe." Her voice sounded edgy, and she couldn't meet his eyes.

He rubbed his hands over his pants, feeling slightly nervous, and bothered by her response.

She turned and looked him in the eye. "How could you sell the house and not tell me?"

He winced, willing to go back in time and tell her everything before she'd heard a rumor from someone else. He'd forgotten that his realtor was best friends with her. "Chloe, I…"

"You've known this for two weeks, Zach," she interrupted, her tone sharp, which was out of character for her. "I knew that at some point you would have to sell the house, and that you're leaving, but you could have at least trusted me enough to…." Her brows pinched, her voice wavered. "I don't know that I would've done anything, but at least you could've told me." She popped her knuckles again, but no sound came out.

Zach reached out to touch her shoulder, to explain that he had turned down the offer. Had her friend told her about the offer, or had she heard rumors from the social media gossip page? "Chloe, that's not exactly the…"

She shook her head, doubt and fear evident in her face. "It's not really about the house… It's about us, Zach."

About us? "I'm sorry, Chloe," was all he could say. "Can we go somewhere and talk about this?"

"We've been talking this entire time, since you came to Eron." She let out an exasperated sigh. "It's best I get used to doing things alone. You're leaving, and then heading to the

Netherlands for another two years. I don't even know what your plans will be after that." Her shoulders sagged and she stared at the empty coffee table. "I need some time to think through things."

She wasn't usually the confrontational type, but apparently that didn't stop her from expressing her feelings with Zach.

Realizing that she wasn't up for negotiating tonight, Zach said, "Please don't overthink." The last thing he wanted was for them to have a conflict when Noah was ready to take her with open arms. "I'll give you some time tonight, but don't take too long…"

The front door bell dinged and Chloe rose immediately. "Enjoy your evening, Zach." She then turned to her customer with a forced smile that the customer would never recognize wasn't genuine.

"How are you doing today?" she greeted her customer.

Zach forced himself to stand, crossed the hardwood floors of the boutique, and stepped outside into the late afternoon sun. Feeling as if someone had just sucker punched him, he forced himself to breathe. This was going to be a long night. He would call her and explain tomorrow, or her friend might update her that he'd turned down the offer before tonight came to an end.

Not that he could blame Chloe for being upset, since he'd withheld the status of his house offer from her. She could have been praying with him, something a couple would do. That, and him not having made it clear that he wanted to spend each passing day with her. He hadn't been bold enough to ask her to go to the mission field with him.

The early June breeze rustled his hair, and he ran a hand through it. A few more days and the town's doctor would resume his duties and Zach would return to LA to spend the final weeks before his trip with his family.

Family. His chest tightened at that word as he remembered the last five minutes he'd spent with Chloe. Chloe was family. He had to make her understand that, because the thought of not having her in his life suddenly created a cloud of darkness.

The brick Noah had tossed landed with a thud on the moist ground. That's exactly how his heart felt, rejected and heavy. Everything around him was darkening, at least that's how he had felt for the last week. Ever since Chloe had told him what he'd already known was coming–that things between them were not going to work out.

Noah tossed a chipped brick to the side, wishing for once that he could leave the town and its gossip behind. He could tolerate the let down by Chloe, but he'd had enough of the social media gossip about him. He longed to get away and come back in two months, after the town had something new and exciting to talk about.

Chloe was a fine woman, sweet and kind. In fact, he'd seen how hard it had been for her to tell him that things would not work out. She'd been sobbing when he left the restaurant, and his heart split in two at the memory.

Noah was standing between her and her happiness with the love of her life. Pain he didn't want to cause her. No doubt she would remain a good friend, and he didn't want to make her feel worse about her honesty.

What could really go worse? He shook his head and reached for another brick from the stack that he was using to build a retaining wall around a home he was working on.

The land around him vibrated with life; from the green grass, to the blooming flowers, and happily chirping birds, yet he felt anything but alive.

His phone rang and he patted his pockets. Pulling it out, he slid a hand out of his glove and squinted at the number. Chloe!

She and Zach had had a falling out, that's what his sister who followed Instagram had told him.

"Hi...uh, Chloe?"

"Sorry to bother you..." Her voice was urgent. "But it's your mom. She was brought into the ER a little while ago, and Zach thinks it might be a heart attack."

Noah blinked and he rubbed his temples with his free hand as Chloe continued. "I'm at the hospital with your dad, and I called your sister, too. They're still running some tests..."

"I'll be right there." He barreled to his truck.

Fifteen minutes later, Noah entered the ER. He breathed in the smell of antiseptic and absorbed the sight of nurses in scrubs bustling in and out of rooms in the small hallway.

Stepping into the waiting room, he found his dad looking frazzled as he ran a hand over his head. The people with his dad stood as Noah approached.

"Any news?"

Chloe shook her head. "Zach will be here soon to give us an update." She walked towards him and enveloped him in a warm embrace. He took comfort in her familiar scent, fresh and clean.

Her eyes were filled with worry, but her words seemed genuine when she whispered, "It's going to be alright."

Noah hoped she was right, because his mom was the heart of the family. He drew strength from Chloe's assurance, despite what had happened between them.

She left and returned shortly with drinks from the vending machines, a Pepsi for Noah, a Sprite for his dad, and Skittles for his sister. He didn't care for anything, but he accepted out of courtesy. "Thanks, Chloe."

Chloe's grandma Jeanie arrived a few minutes later, along with Chloe's dad.

"Any news yet?" George asked Noah's dad, who relayed the information they'd gotten.

Jeanie suggested they pray, and they all bowed their heads to pray for Millie.

As they ended with a collective *Amen*, the doctor showed up. They all rose instantly.

"The bad news is that Millie had a heart attack." Noah's eyes flew open as he waited for Zach to continue. "The good news is that there's not too much blockage in her coronary arteries, and she will not need open heart surgery."

Noah exhaled finally. "So what needs to be done?"

"She will need an angioplasty." He went on to explain what that meant. "It's a procedure done to unblock a blood vessel, especially a coronary artery. After the procedure, a stent will be inserted…"

"Has Garth done that before?" Noah interrupted. The other doctor had just returned from his recovery, and Noah wasn't too confident of the steadiness of the old man's hands.

"Unfortunately, he hasn't. There are two options. You could take her to the facility in Colorado Springs within the next thirty minutes, or I will be glad to do the procedure, since I've done it several times."

As much as Noah wanted to argue with Zach, just out of his personal pride, there was no time to waste. His mom was probably in worse shape than the doctor was letting on.

"Think about it for a few minutes, but remember she needs to be treated right away."

Zach's eyes flew to Chloe, who sat behind them. Longing and pain were evident in the doctor's eyes, and Noah ignored the sting of it all. The doctor turned to leave.

"Let's do the procedure." Noah's dad spoke, and Zach turned.

"The longer we wait, the more we put her life at risk," Noah's sister added.

Noah ran a hand over his eyes and nodded slowly. His family was right. "Yes, let's do it," he whispered.

Time dragged as they sat in the waiting area for hours. Noah's heart lodged in his throat when Zach returned, and the group rose instantly.

Zach looked exhausted but pleased. "Procedure went well."

After they'd shared a group hug, Chloe's grandma planted a soft kiss on Zach's cheek and thanked him.

Chloe thanked Zach without meeting his eyes, then moved back and sank into a chair as Millie's family began asking to see her.

"One at a time. She's still in ICU at the moment," Zach said.

Finally able to breathe, Noah wanted to shake the doctor's hand, but was too proud to do so. "Good thing she didn't die in your operating room," he said instead, hoping Zach understood his joke.

Zach chuckled nervously while accepting a handshake from Noah's dad, who then followed the nurse to the ICU where his mom was located.

This is awkward. Zach was his enemy. Despite his own misgivings, Noah found himself following the doctor down the hallway to thank the man. Another heroic deed from Zach.

Noah outstretched his hand and shook Zach's, his chest tightening. "If you can treat patients as good as you've done in our town, I'm pretty sure that you can win back Chloe without working as hard as I did."

Zach frowned, confused by what Noah was saying. "She's mad at me and I'm leaving!"

"I just complimented you as one of the smartest people I know, so don't make me regret it. If you love her, you will find a way to make things work out."

Zach smiled, brows furrowed curiously, as if trying to figure Noah out.

"You're going to get used to me being nice for a little bit," Noah said.

"It could be a good change of pace," Zach said.

"I gotta go see my mom." He left the doctor's presence knowing that yes, sometimes loving someone meant you needed to let them go.

CHAPTER 17

"**Y**ou shouldn't beat yourself up," Wayne spoke to Zach. The dim twinkling lights caught the silver stubble along the attorney's jaw. "You beat Noah and won the girl. Whatever you two have going on will come to pass."

The last thing he wanted was to discuss Chloe with Wayne, even though he'd become quite friendly with the attorney and his wife after eating at their house a few times. Zach stared at the couple sitting across the table, which had been pushed closer to the wall to clear space for a dance floor, then swung his chin from one to the other. "You two should go and dance."

Wayne gazed at his wife fondly. "You're right. Marcy and I are going to join in the fun." Wayne pushed back his chair and held out a hand to his wife. The heavyset woman pushed back her chair and smiled at her husband while he took her hand in his. They soon mingled with the rest of the couples on the dance floor.

Alone at the table, Zach watched everyone in the center of the room swaying to some song he didn't recognize. His realtor danced with her new husband, keeping her eyes on him alone. The dark skinned man's white teeth gleamed throughout the dance, giving away his emotions. Zach contemplated leaving now that the wedding ceremony was over, especially since Chloe had vanished just as the dancing started.

The outdoor ceremony had been beautiful, with the couple exchanging vows they had written themselves, underneath a white canopy decorated with garlands of eucalyptus and tiny roses. Afterwards, the guests moved inside to one of the spacious rooms on the second floor of the house for the reception. Several flower arrangements adorned the center of each table, and twinkling lights were strung across the room.

The emotions evoked by this whole scene caused Zach to wonder about his own status, and how long it would be before he would get married.

Ten days had passed since he'd been at Chloe's shop, when she'd told him she needed time to think. How long was it going to take for her to think?

In less than three weeks, Zach would be leaving for New Zealand, which left him no time to wait for Chloe to make up her mind about their relationship.

He'd gone to LA intending to stay for over two weeks, but he'd ended up just staying for a little over one week, the same week that Chloe had gone to New York. He'd texted to let her know that he was going home to visit his family, and she'd only responded asking for an address where she could send the check for his trip.

Not one to ever back down, especially with matters involving Chloe Love, Zach had not responded with an address, but instead, he'd still sent her text messages at late hours of the night when he couldn't sleep. He'd asked several times if she was done thinking, and she'd punched him in the face by not responding to either of his messages. Yup, effectively putting him in his place, yet all it created for him was panic–panic that she might be out of his life for good.

That was the reason Zach had flown back last night, so that he could spend the final weeks before he left trying to work things out with Chloe.

He scanned the swaying bodies for Chloe as the need to put an end to this debacle ignited within him. He felt like the odd man out when everyone else, young and old, was dancing.

Probably every girl in town knew that Zach and Chloe were a couple, and they were more loyal to her than to Zach, since they were already blaming him for their separation. Zach could only assume they were bored now, since they didn't have anything to talk about anymore. He couldn't remember what they'd called him on social media, and he hadn't followed the tag since.

Jules emerged, almost unrecognizable without her ponytail. The green dye was gone from her hair, and it was now its natural blonde, cascading down to her shoulders. She sat at the bridal table, where Chloe had been sitting earlier, while they'd caught each other's gazes from time to time across the room. Before she'd disappeared.

Maybe Zach could ask Jules to dance while he waited for Chloe to show up. He assumed nobody else would ask Jules to dance, since she tended to make people believe she was scary.

That's what Zach had believed, too, until two weeks ago, when she'd called him, frantic because she thought a fox on her property was taking its last breath. Zach had assumed that to be the case, but she'd insisted he come check it out before she gave it a proper burial.

Thankfully, he'd gone. The fox had choked on a plastic bag, and as soon as Zach removed it from its throat, the animal had coughed and come back to life before skittering off into the woods. Since then, Zach had reconsidered his opinion about Jules, because no one who cared that much about a stray animal could be that mean.

"Can I dance with you?" He startled and looked up to find a brunette standing beside his table. "That's if you're single."

He hadn't been in town very long, but Zach was familiar with several faces of Eron residents. The brunette looked oddly unfamiliar, and she definitely had no idea about his story with Chloe.

Zach hesitated as he searched for a response. Chloe came to mind, how she'd not returned his texts. He'd been quite jealous seeing her comforting Noah at the hospital, and how carefree she had been with his family. Even if Noah thought that Zach could claim Chloe, he had no idea if Noah had changed his mind and now wanted Chloe back.

"I take it that you're not single?"

Zach blinked and shook his head, the woman's voice pulling him from his thoughts. *One dance wouldn't hurt*, he thought. "I'm single, but not searching. However I would be glad to dance."

It was going to be hard to dance with anybody and not think of Chloe, since they'd practiced one of their dances when they did a dance class. The minute he accepted Brunette's hand, Chloe reappeared from wherever she'd been. Her eyes instantly found Zach's in the crowd.

Brunette said something, maybe introducing herself, but Zach couldn't stop staring at Chloe's party dress that hit below the knee. It was red, the same color as the bridesmaids' dresses, but Chloe had paired hers with beige high heeled sandals.

Brunette kept chattering, something about her cousins, but Zach's mind was far from the dance, especially right now, as he watched Noah approach Chloe and whispered something in her ear before taking her hand in his, leading her to the dance floor.

Zach's stomach churned, burning with jealousy, panic and anxiety. The song played and he danced, or was he staring at Chloe and Noah?

"Looks like someone else has caught your eye and you've changed your mind about searching?" Brunette's eyes followed Zach's to where Chloe danced.

"I'm sorry," he said. "I don't feel like dancing right now." Zach dropped Brunette's hand and turned away, but the woman followed him to a tall, decorative table.

"Let's take a break." She wrapped her hand inside Zach's elbow, and he hated the scene it all painted. He carefully extracted his hand from hers and leaned forward to rest his elbows on the table.

If only he'd turned down the dance with Brunette, he would either be talking or dancing with Chloe right now.

Despite not wanting to dance with anybody but Zach, Chloe hated to turn down Noah's invitation to dance. The least she could do was dance with the man whose heart she'd broken.

Her mind had gone haywire the moment she'd seen Zach at the beginning of the ceremony. She hadn't expected him to return to Eron when he'd texted her during the time of not talking to each other to let her know that he was going to LA to see his family.

When the dancing started, Chloe had offered to help the wedding coordinator put away the wedding gifts, just to give herself time to figure out how to approach Zach after she'd gone all silent on him for several days that seemed like weeks.

Her attention wandered as she and Noah weaved through the other couples, and her eyes found Zach's again. The tan button up shirt she'd custom designed for him made his green eyes pop. His dress pants hung low when he leaned against the tall, round table to talk to Sofia's cousin, a gorgeous brunette who'd flown in for the wedding.

The woman couldn't keep her hands off Zach's arm. At least he had tried to pull his arm free from her a few times, but that didn't stop Chloe from feeling jealous. Yet it was her own fault they were separated.

Chloe had deeper issues to deal with than just Zach leaving. There was the lack of faith that Zach was hers–she still had the fear of abandonment, and the plans Zach had discussed with her didn't reassure her. Zach's plans didn't involve settling down, which meant marriage was far from his radar.

She had to face the reality that Zach had a responsibility to do what God called him to do. What if he wasn't meant to be in a relationship, and Chloe was holding him back from serving God?

He'd said he wanted her in his life, they obviously had chemistry and got along very well, but was that enough?

She loved Zach so much that she would drop everything in Eron to follow him wherever he went. She'd even entertained the idea of what it would be like to go on a mission trip, or to another country and help less fortunate people. She liked the idea of using her gifts to help others, maybe sewing–she could teach people to make their own clothing. But that was all in her thoughts. Even though Zach hadn't invited her along, he'd at least planted a seed in her of helping those in need. Maybe someday she would travel to a third world country and do that.

While in New York for the Black and White banquet, Chloe had stayed busy enough to pretend that she didn't want to respond to Zach's texts, but he was all she could think of. She now regretted dumping him, or at least that's how it must have seemed when he'd pleaded they go somewhere to talk about her outburst and she'd told him she needed time to think.

At the time, it had seemed like a good idea to practice what life would be like with Zach gone. All she felt now was uneasy at the thought of not having him in her life.

She'd really messed up.

She suddenly didn't care whether Zach's future plans involved her or not. What did she want from him when he had already told her that he had no idea what his future looked like? That he wanted to figure things out with her. *Isn't that what God wants us to do anyway? To take one day at a time?*

The slow song continued, and Noah twirled Chloe around, perhaps noticing her absentmindedness. "I decided to go with gray in the sunroom after all," he said.

"Not green?" Chloe teased, since she'd suggested green for his sunroom when he'd asked her.

"Green would be too flashy for me." His smile didn't meet his eyes this time. Chloe ached at the thought that he'd had her in mind when he fixed up his home. "I've always liked gray."

He twirled her around again, and Chloe's eyes shot back in Zach's direction to find him absorbed in whatever the petite woman was telling him. At least it seemed that way to Chloe.

Don't take too long to think. Zach's words rang in her mind. Was he already moving on from her? Her stomach dropped, and she sucked in a quick breath of surprise at how much the sight hurt.

Without warning, Zach's gaze snapped to Chloe. Not searching, but rather as though sensing someone's gaze on him. He'd known exactly where she was and, judging from the dark and wary look on his face, exactly who she was dancing with. His eyes locked on hers for a long moment before the song ended.

When Zach shifted his attention to his pretty companion and bent down to whisper something in her ear, Chloe dropped her hands to turn and leave.

"You're okay?"

Noah's voice reminded her that she had actually had a dance partner, so she masked her battling jealousy and faked a smile. "It's a little warm in here." She fanned herself. "I'm going to go outside and get some fresh air." *And maybe cry a little.*

Noah gave her a concerned look, and he turned in Zach's direction before staring down at Chloe. "Would you like me to come with you?"

"No, thank you."

"I'll be around in case you're up for another dance," he offered, not seeming to take offense at her excuse. Chloe knew he was being polite–he surely had to know that her abrupt departure had everything to do with Zach.

She trotted down to the cobblestone court where the ceremony had been held earlier. The full moonlight was bright enough to light the entire courtyard, which had already been cleared of chairs. She stopped in front of a fountain surrounded with lush plants, daffodils, tulips and a variety of colorful blooms. The sound of water cascading from the fountain relaxed her. Chloe breathed in the crisp air–the breeze wasn't refreshing, but she couldn't care less.

It was hard to hear footsteps over the sound of the fountain, but she sensed someone behind her, close enough that she could feel his breath and knew the scent. Chloe turned and looked up into Zach's face in the moonlight, looking more determined than ever. She felt exhilarated.

"You look perfect tonight...beautiful as always," he said in a gruff voice.

"Thanks." She turned her gaze back to the fountain, afraid she might get tongue tied if she stared at him. "You look handsome, too."

"We need to talk," he said.

"I'm sorry." Chloe knew she'd overreacted. "It was rude of me to not return your texts and calls."

"You do not get to brush me off, Princess." His tone sounded light, and Chloe's gaze flitted from the fountain to him. He had a grin on his face when he pulled her towards him. "It's totally unorthodox."

"That's why I'm apologizing, so..."

Zach bent and brushed his lips against hers lightly, and the rest of her words were lost against his mouth. The light kiss sent shivers through her nerves, the way Zach's kisses often did.

"I missed you," he whispered. Without giving her enough time to respond, he kissed her again. She savored his warmth, his closeness, not caring that their future together was uncertain.

Zach pulled back and rested his forehead on Chloe's. "You know how we always say that cheesecake is not healthy for us?"

She nodded. "Uh huh."

"Ignoring my calls, not talking to you, and knowing that I might not have you in my life, was far worse for my health. Please tell me that you don't intend to ever do that again."

She chuckled, realizing how much she'd missed his humor. "I will try not to." Feeling the need to pour out her heart, she continued, "I don't care if you sold the house and didn't tell me. I don't expect you to spell out your plans, I don't even care to know what lies ahead, because God knows all that. At least I have you today." She sighed. "I want to enjoy each moment that I have with…"

"I want you to have the house and the property," he said, cutting her off.

She stepped back and blinked in surprise.

Zach continued, "I mean, with me. Marry me, Chloe. I want to build lasting memories with you in that meadow. Lasting memories in the family. I can't see anybody there but you. Even if you don't want to marry me, I still want you to keep the house."

"But you're..."

"Yes, leaving, and I want you to come with me."

Her hands flew to her warm cheeks in a vain attempt to cool them down.

"We can get married as soon as possible, I know where we can process your visa and passport within two weeks."

"I have a passport..." She uttered the words so fast.

"That's even better." He pulled her hands from her cheeks and held them in his. "We can have our honeymoon in New Zealand when we're on a mission trip, then come back to our home in Eron, so that—" He stopped his words mid-sentence, perhaps surprised by her silence. "Now would be the time when you say something–anything to put me out of my misery."

She breathed in, then out, unable to contain her joy as she held back tears. "Yes, Zach, yes." She flung her arms around him in a warm embrace. They clung to each other as she laughed and cried at the same time.

For the first time, neither of them seemed to be in a hurry to go anywhere, nor worried about onlookers. Thankfully, everyone was inside dancing...or maybe not, because a loud cheer erupted from the balcony and cameras flashed.

They pulled apart and noticed half the wedding crowd on the balcony, clapping their hands underneath the twinkling lights.

"I guess that's the nature of our town." Zach's voice was resigned, but he was grinning. "I also believe that you owe me a dance."

"Yes, I do." She was looking forward to their first dance, and the way Zach called Eron 'our' town made Chloe's heart soar.

EPILOGUE

1 year later

Pressing his pen firmly on the paper, Zach scrawled in bold, uppercase letters, 'MEET ME IN OUR SPOT.' He taped the note to the front door, where Chloe would be sure to see it as soon as she got home.

Next, he readjusted the crystal vase filled with green and yellow ranunculus that he'd set in the center of the coffee table. He grabbed his guitar from the floor and strapped it to his chest, then picked up the picnic basket from the kitchen counter before strolling away from the house.

Most afternoons, he and Chloe took walks around the meadow and watched the sunset together. Zach had left early so he could surprise his wife with their song, her favorite song. '*Here Comes the Sun.*'

Their first wedding anniversary would be in two days. They had married in Eron a few days before their departure to New Zealand. Instead of the wedding march, 'Here Comes the Sun' had been the song Chloe had chosen for her walk down the aisle.

Chloe had bought several sewing kits and taught several people in the small village in New Zealand how to sew and mend their own clothes. The six months abroad had flown by fast and they returned to Eron, where Chloe's friend Jules had kept the boutique running smoothly. Chloe's clothing lines were now featured in boutiques all over the country.

Zach had turned down the job offer in the Netherlands. Not only did he have a reason to stay in Eron, but Garth had decided to retire the moment Zach and Chloe returned from their trip.

Zach was now the town's doctor. He had also talked Dr. Cami into moving to Eron permanently, so Zach could have the flexibility for him and Chloe to go on mission trips together. They didn't have any specific trips lined up, but had discussed going to Indonesia or Romania next year.

He walked out of the groomed yard and into the tall meadow grass that surrounded the house property. The late summer afternoon was warm, with a light breeze. Bees buzzed in the flowers in the meadow, and the fragrance of flowers filled the air. A perfect afternoon, free of the exhausting demands of work.

Zach spread a plaid blanket on the soft emerald grass, then set the basket on it. He stepped back to admire the hilly landscape around him.

Several minutes later, when he sighted Chloe in the distance, the evening sun glinting gold over her yellow dress, Zach adjusted his guitar and took a few steps towards her. He struck the first chord of his guitar, and Chloe smiled, her smile warm as always.

"Here comes the sun..." Zach joined his voice to his strumming.

Chloe stilled and held his gaze as she listened to him sing the rest of the words. "Oh, honey." She wrapped her arms around him once he set his guitar down. "How did I deserve you?"

"I ask myself the same about you." He kissed her forehead and inhaled the sweet scent, which always warmed him inside. "Hmmm..." he moaned. "You smell like Chloe." He kissed her mouth.

"You smell like Zach," she breathed over his lips. "My favorite smell."

Unable to resist her tantalizing fragrance, he pulled her in for another lingering kiss, which before long became a storm of kissing and touching, food completely forgotten.

"If we keep up with all this touching and kissing, I'm not sure how many babies we will end up having," Chloe giggled.

Lips close to hers, Zach teased, "Who says there's a limit to the number of babies we can have? There's plenty of room for all the little princesses and little princes to roam around this land." His hands found their way into her hair, but just as he was about to kiss her again, she hesitated and stared at him with so much love radiating from her eyes.

"We're going to have a little prince or princess," she whispered.

Zach's eyes widened as Chloe's words registered. "You're pregnant?"

She nodded, smiling when she recognized his grin. He jumped up and raised his arms over his head, then screamed into the open space, "We're going to have a baby!" His voice echoed over the land.

Then he turned to the smiling Chloe and pulled her up, showering kisses on her neck, nose and all-over her face. He lifted her off the ground, and she wrapped her feet around him.

"I love you, Chloe."

"I love you too, Zach."

A moment passed as she looked up at him, the longing he felt inside himself reflected clearly in her eyes.

"Mrs. Eron, you just gave me the best news ever!" He set her down after several seconds of staring at her with such admiration. He leaned over and spoke to her tummy. "Can you hear me, little prince, or are you a princess?" He then touched her tummy. "Is the baby kicking yet?"

She giggled, "You're a doctor, and you very well know that babies haven't developed their boxing hands this early."

He dragged her to the hill, and they sat side by side as they watched the sunset fade away, just like their memories of the past, both contemplating the way life was filled with choices, both easy and difficult, that must be made.

Chloe rested her head on Zach's shoulder and he tightened his grip around her waist, delighting in the fact that their decision to stay in Eron had been the right choice. There was no more doubt, this was the place God wanted them for this season in their lives.

If you enjoyed reading this book, please leave a Review.

Honest reviews by readers like yourself help bring attention to books. A review can be as short or as detailed as you like. Thank you so much!

If you missed the first book in the Eron Outsiders, you can read Sofia and Trevor's story in **COMPLEX**.

COMING SOON!

Noah Buzz will return with his own story in the near future. He still needs some time to recover from losing Chloe. In the meantime, return to Eron for **BEYOND REPAIR,** Book 3 in the Eron Outsiders.

A bitter woman hiding from a troubled past. An ex-con running from a violent gang. Can Jules and Lorenzo find redemption in Eron, or are their lives Beyond Repair?

Hiding from her troubled past, Jules Demski sequesters herself in the mountains of Eron, Colorado, the only place she's ever felt safe. Her solitude is shattered when an injured man staggers into her family's barn.

The last thing she needs is another criminal on her hands. If she can only convince her heart of this, she just might be able to resist the interloper's charm.

Former gangster Lorenzo Macedo has cleaned up his act, but now he's running for his life. He stumbles into a barn just as a bullet pierces his body.

Jules appears standoffish and cold, but the tender way she nurses Lorenzo reveals a soft-hearted, passionate woman aching for her own wounds to be healed. No woman has ever set his blood on fire like Jules, but he has nothing to offer her but a life on the run.

Can two broken people find redemption together?

A NOTE FROM THE AUTHOR

Thank you for reading *CHOICES*. It's always a blessing to meet new readers. And to those who read *COMPLEX*, and all my other books, thanks for giving me another chance, and for your reviews and notes of encouragement.

I enjoyed tapping into Chloe's and Zach's lives in the town of Eron. It may sound strange to some that a small town could be getting carried away with taking people's pictures to post on the community Facebook or Instagram page. I grew up in a small town, where it wasn't necessarily about rumors, but people looked forward to have something new and exciting going on. Especially when new people came into town, that was a good enough reason to peer around and find out all there was about the newcomer.

It was hard for me to put Noah in the position of experiencing unreciprocated love, but sometimes life throws us a curve that makes us stronger in the end. For that reason, Noah will be back to start over with another outsider.

If you would like to check out my other books, please follow me on AMAZON.

God bless you,

Rose Fresquez

ABOUT THE AUTHOR

Rose Fresquez weaves Christian Interracial Romances. She has also written two Family Devotions. She leaves in the Rocky Mountains with her husband and their four children. When she's not busy taking care of her family, she's writing.

You can connect with Rose online at www.rosefreszquez.com

Or look for her on

Facebook

Goodreads

Book Bub.

Twitter

To hear about future releases, subscribe to her Newsletter, which is usually sent out twice a month with free reads from other authors and random drawings just for fun.

Alternatively, email her at rjfresquez@gmail.com

BUCHANAN Series:

FIRST SITE

SOMETHING RIGHT

NEW LIGHT (SHORT STORY)

BONUS CHAPTER-COMPLEX

CHAPTER 1

Detective Trevor Freeman sat in the interview room and wiped the perspiration that threatened to flood his dark skin. He wiggled in his seat to take off his olive green jacket and observed the victim who'd been robbed while working at his uncle's store.

"Aidan, do you have any questions before we proceed?"

"Uh ... I'm good, I guess." Aidan rubbed the back of his neck with his hand.

Trevor rose from his seat and gave the seventeen-year-old a friendly pat on the shoulder. Being only nine years older, Trevor hoped his youthful appearance would put the guy at ease.

"Are you ready to view the lineup of the suspects?"

Aidan nodded his response and followed Trevor to another room.

"Do you see the men who robbed the store?" Trevor asked, while his partner Enrique observed.

Aidan's gaze narrowed as he studied the row of men behind the glass, his fingers tapping on his cheek. He turned to Trevor. "Number two for sure," he said. "He was holding the door with a baseball bat in his hand."

Trevor took a step closer, thankful that this case was coming to an end. "Anyone else?"

Aidan gazed through the glass. "Hmm ... I want to say it's number four," he said, pointing to the guy with long hair dyed in neon colors. "He looks like the dude who jammed the gun in my ribs while I was hanging screwdrivers on the display rods. But he didn't have piercings, or dyed hair."

Trevor and Enrique exchanged looks.

"Let's go with the one with piercings and dyed hair," Trevor spoke, confident that was the guy he needed. He had a gut feeling.

"What if ... he's not the one?" Aidan asked.

"That's not for you to stress about," Trevor said. "We'll bring him in for questioning, and if he's not the one, we'll let him go."

Trevor was ninety-eight percent certain the suspect with dyed hair was one of the robbers. For one thing, he could have just dyed his hair as a disguise. Two, from the way the piercings on his nose were swollen and bleeding it looked as if he'd just gotten that done a few days ago.

Two hours later, after questioning, it turned out that the two suspects knew each other and had robbed the hardware store. It had been easy to get the guy with dyed hair to confess since he panicked when Trevor told him he was going to stay in jail for two years. Trevor had told him if he made it easier by admitting his guilt, his sentence would be shortened.

This had been the second case Trevor had solved this week. He was in a good mood for the rest of the afternoon at work and as he drove home at the end of the day. Since his colleague Enrique had the night shift, Trevor hoped to at least get home in time to get a few things done.

As he drove towards home, Trevor's good mood was interrupted when a red mustang crept over the center-line. Trevor cursed under his breath as he swerved and skidded to a stop.

He pulled his speedometer and clocked the car at fifteen miles over the speed limit. Unfortunately, he knew that car and the driver, since he'd given him a speeding ticket two days ago. Brent Wise, just thinking of the name stirred some memories of his mom that he'd tried to set aside and move on.

Since Trevor's duties as a small-town detective included more than solving mysteries, he sighed and raked a hand through his black, tight curly hair before turning on his red and blue lights to chase after the car.

"Do you know how fast you were going?" Trevor asked when Brent rolled down the window.

"Just give me the darn ticket," Brent snapped. "You think giving me tickets will rectify your mom's disappearance?"

Trevor wouldn't say they'd ever been friends due to more reasons than just the fact that his mom used to be their housekeeper before she went missing.

"I'm going to give you a warning, this time."

Brent's contemptuous gaze lingered on Trevor's feet. "Just give me the ticket. Looks like you could use a new pair of shoes anyway."

Even if Trevor could use a new pair of shoes, that was the least of his concerns at the moment. "You can only get so many tickets before your license is suspended."

"Are we done here?" Brent asked. "Unlike you, I have other important things to do."

Trevor's jaw tightened, and he bit his lip, holding back the words that he wanted to say. He forced himself to wave at Brent and moved back to his SUV, the one the town's people had bought for the police. He had no doubt that the Wise family had contributed some funds as well.

Brent's words bothered him all the way home, stirring up a longing for his mom. Who did the Wises think they were? He pulled into the driveway of his childhood home, the one he'd always known, and which he now shared with his dad Rex and sister Keisha.

As Trevor settled back on his pillow that night, he tossed and turned several times before he pulled himself out of bed. He powered his laptop and went to the kitchen to make himself a coffee. He returned to the living room shortly with a steaming mug and went back to the email his friend Dan, had sent him two weeks ago, with a picture of his mom.

He sat on the couch shuffling through the files on his computer as he nursed a cup of coffee in the dimly lit living room of the three-bedroom house.

By studying at night, he didn't inconvenience his dad, Rex and his sister, Keisha, plus the darkness helped him concentrate. He glanced at the lit clock on the wall. A little after midnight, and if his father knew he was going through these records, he would blow a lid.

His gaze narrowed on the picture in his file of a woman who looked like his mother, studying it with interest. With each click of the mouse and turn of the pages in the case file, he was trying to be as quiet as possible. The last thing he wanted was to wake up his family and face their scrutiny. They didn't exactly approve of the sleepless nights he spent investigating their mother's disappearance.

His dad, Rex did better when it came to the whole 'let bygones be' and leaving vengeance to the Lord. But Trevor did not let things go without putting up a fight. As a new believer, Trevor was starting to let God fight his battles, but that was easier to accept when he didn't think so much of his mom. Besides, he often wondered, wasn't there also a saying that God helped those who helped themselves? Perhaps this was his way of helping himself— seeking justice for his mother.

Dad had told him to lay off the case for a while. He insisted it was consuming Trevor, and that he was becoming obsessed with the case.

His family made it clear that they thought he couldn't do anything with his life because of it, but Trevor had found that idea ridiculous. After all, he was the town's detective. If Trevor helped investigate other cases, why not use the skills for his family's benefit? He could admit that he was obsessed, but who wouldn't be obsessed with finding their mother if she went to work one day and never came back?

He let out a long sigh. Nothing seemed to make sense, and the case had only gotten more complicated. Convinced that his mother, Jayla's employers had something to do with her disappearance, Trevor had filed a lawsuit against them, five years ago. If he could only find enough evidence to make this more of a case than just a made up story he would ....

The Wises thought they were above anyone else who wasn't in their wealthy circle. And that was one thing Trevor couldn't stand.

The arrogance of that family was beyond what he could handle. He couldn't fathom how people could be so careless. They didn't even seem fazed by his mother's disappearance. It was too bad they messed with the wrong person—they would not get away with this. If his suspicions proved correct, he would make sure they paid for their crimes.

After all his mom had done for them, working hard as their housekeeper, for them to not even bat an eye at her disappearance was unsettling. Trevor knew the family was self-centered, but he'd never imagined anyone could be so cold.

Although Trevor may have found himself consumed with the task of solving his mother's case, it was only because he wouldn't be able to live with himself if Jayla became one of those news stories of a woman who went missing without a trace. Whether she was alive or—as much as it pained him to think about it—dead, he needed closure. He was going to get to the bottom of it, regardless of how many toes were stepped on in the process.

"You still looking at mama's case?" a soft female voice asked from somewhere in the darkness.

Trevor raised his head up from the files he had been mulling over. He could just make out the form of his little sister. Her petite figure was leaning against the wall that separated the kitchen from the living room, observing him. Her jet-black hair was knotted into a loose ponytail.

Keisha had been about thirteen years old, and Trevor twenty-one when their mother had disappeared. While Keisha remembered the woman, she probably didn't have as strong of a bond with her as Trevor had. Though she had cried and mourned the absence of their mother, Keisha had long ago come to the conclusion that their mother was dead and was never coming back. A conclusion Trevor refused to subscribe to about the mother he remembered so well.

The detective side of him knew that something had likely gone wrong with his mom, but this wasn't just a case of a stranger gone missing. This was his mom! There had been many cases over the years of people being held hostage for years. She could still be alive.

His gaze briefly returned to the picture in his hand, and he considered putting it back in the file so he could look it up another day. "Yes, Ki," he finally responded. "What's up?"

"Felt thirsty, came to get some water, and almost thought I wouldn't find you still awake, but you're always up late, doing the same thing." She offered a weak smile. "Disappoint me for once, Trev."

Keisha might have rolled her eyes at the end of her sentence but the light was too dim for Trevor to see her eyes. He shook his head, letting her words slide off. She was starting to sound too much like their father these days.

"You had your water?" he asked, effectively dismissing anything else she had said. He wasn't going to engage her in this argument at such a late hour. Besides, whenever he did have this argument, it never led to a resolution. Only frustration for both parties.

Keisha was silent for a while, but Trevor waited for her response.

"Yes," she responded reluctantly. However, he didn't miss the slight defiance in her voice. Trevor could read his sister better than he could read anyone else. He'd taken care of Keisha since she was a baby, from helping his mom change her diapers to entertaining her. He'd watched her grow from infancy to the full teenager she was, and when their mother went missing, he had more or less taken over part of the parenting role alongside his dad.

Trevor was a lot like a second parent, and his knowledge of Keisha was just as apt as any parent would have of their child. He knew she wanted to help him. She meant well. They all did.

"Goodnight Ki, you better get to bed." he said gently, dismissing her.

Once again, she stood silent for a minute longer before making any action, and then turned. "You might want to consider your own advice and catch some sleep," she spoke over her shoulder. "Your endless worrying is catching up on you." Keisha offered those last parting words before disappearing into the shadows from where she'd emerged.

Trevor looked at the file in his hands, only this time, he wasn't really seeing the pictures, just staring at them as he thought of Keisha's words. He wiped his hands across his heavy eyes, closed up the file, and tossed it onto the coffee table with a grunt. He gulped the rest of the coffee in his cup. It was a hopeless effort, as Keisha might have rolled her eyes at the end of her sentence but the light was too dim for Trevor to see her eyes. He shook his head, letting her words slide off. She was starting to sound too much like their father these days.

"You had your water?" he asked, effectively dismissing anything else she had said. He wasn't going to engage her in this argument at such a late hour. Besides, whenever he did have this argument, it never led to a resolution. Only frustration for both parties.

Keisha was silent for a while, but Trevor waited for her response.

"Yes," she responded reluctantly. However, he didn't miss the slight defiance in her voice. Trevor could read his sister better than he could read anyone else. He'd taken care of Keisha since she was a baby, from helping his mom change her diapers to entertaining her. He'd watched her grow from infancy to the full teenager she was, and when their mother went missing, he had more or less taken over part of the parenting role alongside his dad.

Trevor was a lot like a second parent, and his knowledge of Keisha was just as apt as any parent would have of their child. He knew she wanted to help him. She meant well. They all did.

"Goodnight Ki, you better get to bed." he said gently, dismissing her.

Once again, she stood silent for a minute longer before making any action, and then turned. "You might want to consider your own advice and catch some sleep," she spoke over her shoulder. "Your endless worrying is catching up on you." Keisha offered those last parting words before disappearing into the shadows from where she'd emerged.

Trevor looked at the file in his hands, only this time, he wasn't really seeing the pictures, just staring at them as he thought of Keisha's words. He wiped his hands across his heavy eyes, closed up the file, and tossed it onto the coffee table with a grunt. He gulped the rest of the coffee in his cup. It was a hopeless effort, as the coffee had been ineffective in blocking his exhaustion, but drinking the bitter liquid had become part of his ritual.

Turning off the lights, Trevor made his way to his bedroom. Keisha was right—he barely got any sleep these days, and his exhaustion was catching up to him. Sleepless nights poring over his mother's case and preparing for the trial left him tired at work in the mornings. He just needed this case solved. Six years was too long to be put through this level of emotional torture and pain. He needed his mother back, and a specific member of the Wise family in jail for abducting her.

Made in the USA
Columbia, SC
20 March 2022

57915947R00167